SPECIAL MESSAGE TO READERS

THE ULVERSCROFT FOUNDATION
(registered UK charity number 264873)
was established in 1972 to provide funds for
research, diagnosis and treatment of eye diseases.
Examples of major projects funded by
the Ulverscroft Foundation are:-

- The Children's Eye Unit at Moorfields Eye Hospital, London
- The Ulverscroft Children's Eye Unit at Great Ormond Street Hospital for Sick Children
- Funding research into eye diseases and treatment at the Department of Ophthalmology, University of Leicester
- The Ulverscroft Vision Research Group, Institute of Child Health
- Twin operating theatres at the Western Ophthalmic Hospital, London
- The Chair of Ophthalmology at the Royal Australian College of Ophthalmologists

You can help further the work of the Foundation
by making a donation or leaving a legacy.
Every contribution is gratefully received. If you
would like to help support the Foundation or
require further information, please contact:

THE ULVERSCROFT FOUNDATION
The Green, Bradgate Road, Anstey
Leicester LE7 7FU, England
Tel: (0116) 236 4325

website: www.foundation.ulverscroft.com

INCIDENT AT ELK HORN

When bounty hunter Gustavus Greeley rides into Elk Horn, he learns that Marshal Detmeyer has failed to return from investigating a shooting at the nearby Baker farm. Riding out to the farm, Greeley finds Mr and Mrs Baker and their son dead, Detmeyer badly wounded, and their two daughters missing. Arrows have been used, and the girls are presumed to be captives of the Apaches — but are they really responsible? Or are brothers David and Will Preston, newcomers to Elk Horn looking for land to take up ranching, somehow involved?

STEVEN GRAY

INCIDENT AT ELK HORN

Complete and Unabridged

LINFORD
Leicester

First published in Great Britain in 2016 by
Robert Hale
an imprint of The Crowood Press
Wiltshire

First Linford Edition
published 2019
by arrangement with
The Crowood Press
Wiltshire

A catalogue record for this book is available
from the British Library.

ISBN 978–1–4448–4273–9

Published by
F. A. Thorpe (Publishing)
Anstey, Leicestershire

Set by Words & Graphics Ltd.
Anstey, Leicestershire
Printed and bound in Great Britain by
T. J. International Ltd., Padstow, Cornwall

This book is printed on acid-free paper

1

Gustavus Greeley rode into Elk Horn in bad need of a bath, a haircut and shave, and a woman. In that order. It was a long time since he'd been without all four.

Once he'd collected the reward for bringing in Matty Scales he'd not only have enough money to pay Madame Josephine for the first three but, after he was clean, he could enjoy the bed and charms of Melissa Fyfield. She was the best girl at Josephine's brothel, and one with whom Greeley was sort of in love.

Elk Horn was an ever-growing town. It existed to serve the ranchers and farmers who made a living in the plains to the south and the valleys and hills to the north. There was even talk of the railroad putting in a spur line. Greeley rode in from the south, as Scales had tried to escape to Mexico, and had nearly made it, too. First came the small business area, then, passing the turning to the red-light district, he reached the heart of the town.

It was nearing that time of day when the stores closed for business, and Main Street was quiet. A few people were still about but most had already headed home for dinner.

The marshal's office, as well as a new courthouse, was situated at the far end of the street. Greeley always reckoned that it would make better sense if they'd been built near the red-light district because it was there most of the trouble occurred. But as he wasn't on the town council no one had asked his advice.

He pulled the two horses to a halt, dismounted and stretched, easing the kinks out of his back. He tied the reins to the hitching rail and stepped up on to the sidewalk.

The deputy marshal, Eddie Smith, looked up expectantly at his entrance.

'Oh, it's you,' he said. He sounded disappointed and despondent.

Greeley took off his Stetson, banging it hard against his knee.

'Who were you expecting?'

'Marshal Detmeyer.'

Making himself at home, Greeley poured coffee out for them both and sat down in Detmeyer's chair, leaning back and eyeing Eddie. He was a tall and gangly youth, with spots, and hadn't been a deputy for long. His eagerness almost made up for his inexperience, but not always; right now he looked very worried.

'What's wrong?'

Something was for sure.

Also it concerned Marshal Detmeyer.

Marshal Detmeyer didn't approve of bounty hunters, whom he accused of only being interested in the reward money. He'd always adhered to and abided by the law and he liked outlaws to stand trial and be sentenced by the judge to be hanged after the jury found them guilty. He most certainly didn't approve of Greeley, who more often than not brought in those he went after dead rather than alive.

The marshal wouldn't like the fact that Matty Scales was dead, his body slung over the back of Greeley's horse.

But hell! What choice did Greeley have when the likes of Scales drew down on him but to shoot back? It wasn't his fault that he was fast on the draw and accurate in his shot.

Anyway, Scales had killed two innocent bystanders during a bank robbery and that was too close to home for Greeley to feel any sympathy towards him.

His being willing to shoot outlaws wasn't the only reason Detmeyer disapproved of Greeley. Gus was twenty-seven, six feet tall and lean-bodied. With his black curly hair, black moustache and blue eyes, he was attractive to women. That included Detmeyer's daughter Ann, who, now she was sixteen and verging on womanhood, was smitten. The fact that Greeley had never encouraged her and never would made no difference. As far as the marshal was concerned, Greeley was at fault and a danger to the girl's virtue.

But Detmeyer was a good man and Greeley was as worried as Eddie. Eddie gulped down some coffee.

'Earlier this afternoon, a farmer called here to say that on his way into town he was passing near to the Baker place when he heard the sound of shooting and smelt smoke.'

'Didn't he stop to find out what was going on?'

'No. He had his wife and two baby sons with him and he was afraid of them getting hurt. Besides I don't think his wife would've let him stop. Instead he drove the buckboard into town as fast as he could to tell us. The marshal immediately rode out to the Baker farm.' Eddie cast a nervous glance at the clock on the wall. 'That was over three hours ago. He should be back by now.'

'How far is it to the farm? Where do they live?'

'In Five-Mile Valley.'

Greeley nodded. He knew where that was.

'It's less than an hour's ride and the marshal would probably have done it even quicker because he was anxious over what the shooting meant.'

Under two hours to get there and back, that left more than an hour to discover the reason for the shootings. Too long? Maybe.

'Perhaps the reason for the gunfire was serious enough to make him stop at the farm to sort it out,' Greeley suggested.

'Could be,' Eddie agreed doubtfully.

The marshal was a conscientious man. Knowing that his deputy would be worried about him, he wouldn't delay there any longer than he had to.

'Why didn't you go with him? Or ride out after him to find out if he was all right?'

'Because, Mr Greeley, you might not realize it, having been gone for a while, but it's Saturday. Cowboys and farmhands have been drifting in all day and even though it's still early I've already had to break up one fight at The Antlers.'

Hell! That was another reason for Detmeyer to get back as soon as he could. He wouldn't want to leave Eddie by himself to handle rowdy and drunken cowboys on a Saturday night.

'I don't think I know the Bakers,' Greeley said.

'No, I don't either, not really. They only get into Elk Horn now and then.'

Greeley nodded again. As farmers, working hard and long hours, day in and day out, all year round, they would only come to town to sell produce and buy those essentials they couldn't grow or rear. Maybe to attend a social dance or a church picnic.

That could, and should, have been his life too.

'I . . . er . . . well, I suppose, Mr Greeley,' Eddie began nervously, 'you wouldn't ride out there and see what's happened, would you?'

Hell! Riding out to investigate a shooting was the last thing Greeley

7

wanted right now.

Not only did he want a rest, he was hungry. He'd existed on crackers and jerky and warm water for too long and he wanted a decent meal: beef-stew and potatoes followed by apple pie — washed down by a couple of beers. He could go to the café for the former and The Antlers saloon for the latter because, say what you liked about Jack Phillips, he served a good, ice-cold beer. Eddie must have sensed his reluctance.

'I can't very well leave here and, well . . . er . . . you might be right about the marshal sorting things out, but equally he could be hurt. Do you think he is? I don't like to think that but I'm afraid he is. Supposing he is — hurt, that is — and he's alone and waiting for help to arrive and — '

'All right!' Greeley interrupted the deputy's gabbling. He stood up to pour himself some more coffee.

Hell! But Eddie's fear was understandable. Shots had been fired earlier, something had been on fire. Both of which could mean only one thing: trouble! Detmeyer had ridden out alone. He could have ridden right into the middle of that trouble, and found it too much to handle by himself.

Greeley might be tired and dirty, he might be hungry and longing for the comfortable arms of a woman but, hell, what choice did he have? He'd never forgive himself if, by doing nothing, Detmeyer's situation became worse. Anyway he wouldn't be able to enjoy anything, not even Melissa's bed, all the while he didn't know if the marshal was all right or not. He sighed, thinking about another long ride ahead of him.

'OK, yeah, I'll go.'

'Thank you, Mr Greeley.' Eddie's face lit up with a relieved smile.

'In the meantime, Eddie, I've got a dead outlaw outside. See he gets to the undertaker for me, and take the two horses to the livery.'

Greeley's horse was as weary as he was; he would have to hire a fresh animal.

'Sure thing.' Unlike his boss, Eddie had no trouble with dead outlaws.

'And have my reward money waiting for me for when I get back!'

2

On an eager-to-be-ridden mare Greeley made good time. Luckily there was a reasonable road for him to follow, as several small farms were situated in the same area, making the way fairly well travelled. It took him first up into the foothills, trees gathering close on either side, before veering away towards Five-Mile Valley.

As he rode along he wondered what his life would have been like as a farmer. It was something he seldom allowed himself to think about because it brought back memories of everything he'd lost.

⋆ ⋆ ⋆

He was thirteen when his father decided to uproot his family — wife, three sons and two daughters — from their farm in Ohio and move West. That was in 1866, shortly after the end of the War Between the States, in which his father had fought for the North. His father said there were lots of opportunities in the new lands being opened up to settlers, more money to be made, good pastures for the taking.

It hadn't quite turned out as easy as that. Arizona proved to be a raw and dangerous place with little in the way of civilization. The work needed to clear the land, build a home and keep it all was tough and relentless. Lonely too. His younger brother had left home as soon as he could and had never been back, and one of his sisters was now a schoolteacher in Flagstaff, having been unable to cope with the solitude.

Yet somehow they had prospered. More people moved into the area. With his eldest brother due to inherit the farm, Gus had started to think of buying some land for himself. Near the family farm but far enough away for him to remain independent. Find a girl to marry and have a family of his own. It was what he wanted.

Then, when he was twenty, everything changed.

One morning his father rode to a local trader's store to buy chewing tobacco. It was something he'd often done before. That day he was in the wrong place at exactly the wrong time. He'd walked through the door while the store was being held up. He'd been shot dead, left to lie in his own blood on the earthen floor.

The outlaw escaped with two dollars and some loose change in his pocket. He'd never been caught.

Overnight Greeley quit the farm to chase after the man who'd widowed his mother. At the same time he decided to become a bounty hunter. He wasn't exactly sure why he did, nor why that and not a lawman, except that suddenly, desperately, he needed to be free, without having to obey other people's rules, to do whatever it took to make those who broke the law pay; with their lives if necessary.

With practice he quickly became a good enough shot — and ruthless enough too — to make a decent living at what he did. His one regret was that he hadn't caught the bastard who'd taken his father's life. But he would never, ever give up looking for him. One day he would find him and then, by God, he'd kill him.

* * *

It was dusk, shadows lengthening all around, when he came to the track that led to the Bakers' farm. As he got closer he realized it was ominously quiet, while a slight smell of smoke remained lingering on the air.

He'd seen no sign of the marshal or his horse on the ride and he'd followed the quickest way to the farm. He couldn't think of any reason why Detmeyer wouldn't have done the same.

It didn't bode well and he approached the place cautiously.

The farm was quite substantial with a large one-storey wooden cabin off to one side. It had several windows and a porch in front. Logs were stacked against one wall. Beyond the yard out front were several work buildings and what had once been a barn but was now a still-smouldering ruin. The yard itself had been churned up by the hoofprints of several horses.

No one was about.

No, this didn't look good at all.

Greeley dismounted beside what remained of the barn. He stood still for a moment or two, taking in the scene. From a shed he heard the lowing of a cow. That was all.

'Hallo,' he called.

No reply. He stepped out into the open.

'Hallo, the house. Anyone there?'

Nothing.

'I'm coming in. I'm no threat to you.'

With hands held away from his sides so no one would think he was going for his gun, he started to walk very slowly towards the house.

He reached the porch without being challenged and stepped up on to it. From somewhere close by something banged. Heart skipping a beat, he swung towards the noise, hand going to his gun. It was just a loose shutter on the nearest window.

Now, not knowing what he would find inside and fearing the worst, he drew his gun and cocked the trigger, wanting to be ready.

With his other hand he pushed at the door. It opened readily.

'Hallo,' he called again before going inside.

Straight away he knew what was wrong. The buzzing of flies was loud and persistent and he wrinkled his nose against the metallic smell of blood.

The place was in a mess. All the chairs were knocked over. The table was on its side, one leg broken. Plates were smashed on the floor. Rag rugs lay higgledy-piggledy where they'd been thrown.

And — oh God — there were the bodies of the Baker family.

Mr Baker lay by the window whose shutter was broken loose. His wife was over by the inner door as if she'd been trying to escape. She was on her side. Near to her was a boy of about seventeen. He must be their son. He lay on his stomach, arms flung out towards his mother, either in an effort to protect her or maybe in a plea for her help.

That they were dead was obvious. It was equally obvious what had killed them. Not bullets but arrows! They were shot through with arrows. Three in Baker's chest. Two in Mrs Baker's back. Two in the boy — one in his leg, the other in his side.

Arrows!

Indians! Apaches!

These days not much scared Greeley. But now all at once his mouth turned dry and his heart started hammering with fear. In the not too distant past this area had been home to several tribes of Apaches who'd raided and killed and tortured until finally being defeated and placed on reservations. Now they had gone on the rampage again.

Were the Indians still around? How many of them had there been? Would they attack him too?

He gave himself a little shake. Of course they weren't still here. Indians attacked and rode away. They would be long gone.

Not that he knew a great deal about Indians.

Growing up on the family farm in the north of the territory, the only time he'd seen Indians up close was when two Navajos called at the house to beg for food. They were old, dejected and dirty. They certainly hadn't posed a threat. Except . . . well . . . what they'd really been after was whiskey but Gus's father wasn't about to let them have that, not wanting to take a risk however harmless they looked. Instead he'd given them food and water and sent them on their way. They hadn't come round again.

Quickly he went through the other rooms in the house. There was a lot more damage but thankfully no more bodies.

And still no sign of Marshal Detmeyer.

Greeley went back outside, gulping in some fresh air. Had the marshal arrived when the raid was taking place? Or had he taken off after the murderers, hoping to capture them and bring them to justice? It was doubtful he would do that, not when he was alone. Detmeyer was a good lawman. He would want those who had done this caught. But he wasn't stupid or foolhardy.

As he stood there wondering what to do next a buzzard flew by overhead and circled round. It was quickly joined by another.

Hell!

They could smell blood and decay.

With a hollow feeling of dread in the pit of his stomach, Greeley jumped off the porch and crossed the yard to the work buildings at the back of the house.

He came to a halt.

There, lying face down on the dusty ground, an arrow sticking out of his back, was Marshal Detmeyer.

He lay unmoving.

'Sam!'

3

'It ain't fair,' Pete moaned. He stared moodily into the embers of the small campfire and drank the last of the coffee, throwing the dregs on to the ground. 'We should be in Elk Horn right now, not out here nurse-maiding a bunch of cows.'

His friend, Mike, nodded glum agreement.

Elk Horn on a Saturday night meant getting drunk, on either beer or whiskey depending on their mood and how much money they had in their pockets, and maybe a game of cards. Preferably a dance or two with a girl in one of the saloons and, if they were real lucky and still had enough money left after all that, the chance to enjoy the favours of a prostitute. Not that that happened very often, although they liked to boast that it did.

Instead the two young cowboys were sitting out here, in the dark and cold night on their own.

They worked for the CW Circle ranch, where the foreman was fair but strict. What he said went. One day he'd said that because they were short-handed due to a couple of the hands suffering accidents, Pete and Mike would have to forgo a trip to Elk Horn and instead help guard the herd. This they had now been doing for almost a week.

They were lonely, tired, thirsty and disgruntled.

'There's always next week I guess.' Mike tried to look on the bright side. 'And someone'll be by tomorrow so we can go back to the ranch. Have something decent to eat and sleep in a proper bed.'

'Yeah, and . . . what was that?'

'What?'

'I thought I heard something. Up there.' Pete pointed to the top of the hill, beneath whose slope they'd made camp. 'Listen.'

'I can't . . .'

Then they both heard it. Stones slithering down the hill towards them. One of their horses snickered and stamped its feet.

'Must be an animal,' Mike said but his hand went to the butt of his gun all the same. Animals out here could be dangerous. Especially those that roamed at night.

All at once the quiet of the black night was broken by shrill yips and yells.

'What the hell is that?' Pete cried in fright, leaping to his feet.

It certainly wasn't an animal.

'It sounds like Apaches.' A shiver of fear ran through Mike.

'It can't be.' Pete looked round at his friend, eyes wide-open with horror. 'Not these days. No!'

Whoosh!

An arrow landed, quivering, in the ground in front of their feet.

Swearing wildly, Mike kicked out at the fire, so its light wouldn't make them an easy target. At the same time Pete pulled his gun from its holster and grabbed Mike's arm, starting to pull him back into the shelter of the hill.

Too late. More arrows were fired at them. One hit Mike in the leg. He screamed in shock and pain and collapsed to the ground out in the open, forcing his friend to let him go.

Yelling, Pete aimed his gun and fired several times in the direction of the hilltop. He had little hope of actually hitting anything because it was too dark to see what he was shooting at.

All the time those yips kept coming. Were they getting nearer? It was hard to tell.

Somehow Mike dragged himself over to his friend. This time Pete succeeded in pulling him into the shadows. There Mike clutched at his leg and moaned.

'Can you see 'em?' he asked.

'No.'

'We're gonna die.'

For some moments Pete said nothing. He very much feared the same.

Goodness knew how many of the bastards were out there. His fevered imagination told him it must be hundreds. If they succeeded in getting close they would easily overpower the two of them. Then he spoke.

'Let's take some of 'em with us.' A forlorn hope as neither man was a good shot.

Then, as suddenly as it had started, the attack stopped.

Everything went quiet.

'Have they gone?' Mike asked after a minute or two. He was unable to believe that they had; rather, he feared that the Indians were even now creeping down the hillside towards them, scalping-knives at the ready.

'I don't know,' Pete whispered. He took the opportunity to reload his gun, almost dropping several bullets on the ground because his hands were shaking so badly.

Trembling, they waited in the dark, certain that at any moment the Indians would rush them.

Nothing.

'They must have left,' Pete said at last. 'Don't know why.' He shrugged. 'Mebbe they was just funning us.'

'My leg don't feel funny.' Mike gave a little moan. 'It hurts like hell. And it's bleeding real bad. I'm gonna bleed to death.'

'No you ain't! We'll wrap our bandannas round the wound to stop the bleeding and then get on into town. Let Doc Hooper have a look at you.'

'Shouldn't we go back to the ranch? Warn them?'

'Elk Horn is nearer. We can get a drink there too.' The ranch was strictly teetotal.

Mike nodded. He could sure do with a whiskey or two.

'And the folks there need to know what's going on too.'

Indians!

4

'Sam!'

Greeley ran over to the stricken marshal, dropped to his knees in the dust beside him. He reached out and gently turned the man on to his side. Then he sighed in relief. Detmeyer was alive. Just. Was still breathing, although his face was ashen and he'd lost a lot of blood: his shirt was soaked in it. He was also icy cold.

Quickly Greeley took off his coat and laid it over the man. He had to get him back to town as quickly as possible so that Doctor Hooper could look after him. The doc was good at what he did; if anyone could save Detmeyer it would be him. But first he had to remove the arrow and do his best to stop the bleeding.

He got to his feet, went back inside the farmhouse and into the kitchen. Here he flung open drawers and cupboards until he found a couple of clean towels. The wound should be washed as well, but he decided he couldn't take the time for that.

Back with the marshal, he turned him on his stomach again. Detmeyer groaned. Gritting his teeth as well as his resolve, Greeley took hold of the shaft of the arrow. One . . . two . . . three . . . he pulled as hard as he could. To his relief the arrow came away fairly easily, making an unpleasant sucking sound as it did so. It was followed by spouts of blood. Detmeyer groaned again. Greeley looked at the arrow. Thank God, none of the arrowhead had been left behind. It was all out. He flung it away.

Shaking a little, he placed one towel against the wound, grimacing as it reddened straight away. He then wrapped the second towel around Detmeyer's back and chest, securing it as tightly as he could. He placed his coat over him again.

Next was the problem of how to get him back to town.

The marshal's horse was nowhere around. Either it had run away or, more likely, the Apaches had taken it. Two horses remained grazing in the nearby meadow but Greeley could tell they were farm horses; used for pulling the buckboard, not for riding. Neither was there any sign of a saddle or bridle. Either the Bakers didn't own such things, or they had gone up in smoke in the barn along with the buckboard.

The unconscious Detmeyer wouldn't be able to ride by himself, anyway.

No, he must get the marshal up into the saddle with him and hold him there. Not ideal and not easy but he had no choice.

Greeley collected the mare. Luckily she was a steady animal, taking no notice of the smell of blood. With some difficulty, as the man was a dead weight, he hauled Detmeyer to his feet and then, with even more difficulty and a lot of cursing, got him up and into the saddle. Detmeyer slumped forward and the wound started bleeding again, but there wasn't much he could do about that. Clutching Detmeyer's body, holding him in place so he didn't slip and fall, he managed to scramble up behind him, whispering to the mare so she would stand still and not dance away.

He'd done it.

His feet in the stirrups and clutching Detmeyer firmly, he kicked the mare into a walk and left behind the farm and the bodies. They were dead. Nothing could be done for them but he could do his damnedest to save Sam.

Despite wanting to reach Elk Horn as soon as possible he didn't dare let the mare go any quicker than a fast walk for fear of jolting Detmeyer's body. The journey seemed to take for ever. Riding into town he avoided the red-light district where people would still be out and about, not wanting anyone to realize the marshal was hurt and start asking questions, wasting time. As he approached the marshal's office, he was thankful to see Eddie Smith jump off the sidewalk and race towards him.

'Mr Greeley!' Eddie caught hold of the horse's reins. 'Oh no, is the marshal dead? What happened? Oh God!'

'Sam's still alive,' Greeley said. 'I'm going to take him home. But he is badly hurt. He was shot with a bow and arrow.'

Eddie gaped at him, looking stunned. 'What? That's impossible.'

'It's true. And the Baker family are dead. Killed the same way.'

Eddie looked as if he was about to faint or vomit.

'I don't believe this,' he managed to say. 'Indians? No.' He shook his head.

'So, Eddie, what I want you to do — and right now — is fetch Doctor Hooper to the marshal's house. And then,' he called back the deputy who was already turning away, 'send telegrams to all the towns round about and to Fort Myerson, warning them that Apaches have broken out of the Reservation and are out raiding.'

'Oh God!'

'Does Miss Ann know something is wrong?'

Eddie nodded. 'Yeah, I thought she

31

ought to be told.' He blushed. He was scared of girls in general and particularly Ann Detmeyer because she was so pretty and nice, always ready with a smile. But realizing she would want to know what was happening, he'd screwed up his courage to go and tell her. 'She's waiting for news.'

'Good. Go on then, quick! You're the town's deputy marshal. Act like it.' This was no time for sympathy. 'Can you do that?'

'Yes, sir,' Eddie stammered a reply. He raced away to carry out Greeley's orders.

*　*　*

The Detmeyers lived on the far edge of town in a wide, pleasant street near the river. They owned a fairly large house, kept neat and clean by Ann. It had a veranda running along the front on which Detmeyer spent most of his free time in a rocking chair, and a yard surrounded by a picket fence. Dr Hooper lived near by, as did the bank manager and most of the town's other wealthier citizens.

Ann was already on the veranda, waiting.

She was turning into a pretty girl, who must take after her mother. Her hair was fair, whereas Detmeyer's was dark brown, and her eyes were a much lighter brown than his. Her cheeks were plump and she still had a girlish figure. Greeley knew that her mother had died of a fever ten years ago and that Sam had never once considered remarrying.

'Papa?' Her voice was uncertain.

'It's all right,' Greeley said at once. Her hand went to her throat. 'Doctor Hooper is on his way. Can you help me get your pa inside?' When Ann nodded and reached up to her father, he saw that her hands were unsteady and she had tears in her eyes. He repeated that it was all right, hoping that it was, and hoping that Hooper would arrive quickly.

With Greeley bearing most of the weight, together they managed to get

Detmeyer into the house and carried along to his bedroom that overlooked the tiny garden at the rear. Greeley lifted him on to the bed and Ann covered him with a blanket.

'Oh, Papa,' she said again in a small, terrified voice.

'See, Ann, the wound has stopped bleeding. That's a good sign. Now, while we wait, why don't you boil up some water and get some towels? And have you got any bandages?'

'Yes.' Ann looked at her father, lying so still in the bed, his breathing uncertain.

'Don't cry.' Greeley put a comforting hand on her shoulder. 'Do what you can to help the doctor. Ah, that sounds like him now. Doc, we're in here.'

Hooper was in his early fifties. He looked exactly like the reasonably well-to-do and highly competent doctor that he was; respected and well thought of by the community. Taking off his jacket and rolling up his sleeves, he immediately took charge. However, even he paused with shock when, in examining his patient, he saw that he was dealing with an arrow wound rather than one made by a bullet.

'What the hell?' he said, glancing at Greeley.

'I know.'

'I don't need you, Gus. Nor you, Ann. No, that's an order. Get me water and bandages and then go and sit down.'

'I'll stay with you,' Greeley promised the girl. On the way to the parlour he collected Detmeyer's bottle of whiskey and two glasses from the kitchen. He poured out a slug for each of them, giving one to Ann when she came in and sat beside him on the sofa.

'Here, that'll help.' The whiskey certainly helped him.

Only a little later Eddie Smith arrived at the house. As usual his face turned beetroot as he saw Ann. Taking off his hat and stammering in her presence even though he was talking to Greeley, he said:

'I've just come from the telegraph office. The operator can't send out any messages, he says, as the wires have been cut.'

'Hell! When?'

'He doesn't know for sure as he hasn't had any messages to send since early this morning and nothing has come in for a while, which of course it wouldn't iffen the wires were cut.' Eddie was aware he was gabbling again and stopped to take a deep breath. 'He also says that's exactly what Apaches do when they're out on a raid, in an effort to avoid capture.'

Before anyone could say anything more, Hooper came in, wiping his hands on a clean towel. They all turned to look at him expectantly. Ann giving a little cry and clutching at Greeley's hand. The doctor smiled in an attempt to reassure them.

'I've cleaned and bandaged the wound. It's not bleeding any more. There's no sign of infection or fever. I think he'll be OK. He's pretty tough, you know.'

'Oh, thank goodness.' Ann began to cry. Hooper took her into his arms and held her close, patting her back.

'But, Gus, what on earth is going on? Surely Apaches haven't started to raid again? Not round here. Not after all this time. We haven't had any real trouble apart from an odd bit of rustling since they went on the Reservation.'

'It certainly looks as if they have.' Greeley told them what he'd found out at the Baker farm.

'Good God!' Hooper said. 'They were all dead?' He ran a hand through his hair. 'You sure?'

'Absolutely. Mr and Mrs Baker. And a young lad. Their son I suppose.'

'Frank is his name,' Eddie put in.

Ann pulled away from the doctor, a startled, very scared look on her face. She glanced from one to other of them.

'But, Mr Greeley, the Bakers had two daughters. Weren't they there? Where are they?'

5

'What!' Greeley said in horrified surprise. 'Are you sure?'

'Of course I am.'

'There was no one else there. I looked all over.'

'Their names are Claire and Rachel,' Ann went on, sounding indignant as if accusing Greeley of not believing her. 'Claire is fifteen and Rachel a year younger. I don't know them very well but they're nice girls.'

'Miss Ann is right,' Eddie agreed, blushing again.

'Those damn Apaches must've taken them.' Greeley leapt to his feet. 'I'll have to go after them.'

'No.' Hooper stood in front of him.

Greeley's eyes flashed and his hands curled into fists. 'But I must. They could still be alive or . . . ' He came to a halt, not wanting to go into detail about what might be happening to them in front of Ann.

'Don't be foolish.' Hooper stood his ground. 'Think about it. It's dark out there. You ride back to the farm now you could easily have an accident. And you won't be able to find any tracks or do anything until morning. Whatever is going to happen to those girls will have been done already.'

'But . . . '

'Not only that but you look worn out. You need something hot and substantial to eat and a good night's rest. You'll be better able to cope then. You go out now you won't be able to function properly. You could place yourself, and the girls, in unnecessary danger.'

Very reluctantly Greeley agreed with the doctor. His stomach was growling with hunger and he felt bone weary.

'OK I'll ride out first thing in the morning.'

'D'you want me to come with you?' Eddie said.

'No.' Greeley shook his head. 'You'd

be best staying in town, taking messages and making sure that folks here don't get too stirred up or get in my way.'

'All right.' Eddie paused, before adding hesitantly, 'But there is someone here in Elk Horn whose help you might like to have. In the circumstances that is.'

'Oh, who?'

'Henry Walsh.'

Greeley had never heard of him, although obviously Hooper had if the nod of agreement he gave was anything to go by.

'He used to be an Indian scout and he says he knows an awful lot about Indians and their ways. He's been retired for a long while now but I reckon he'd still be good at tracking an' such. Anyway he's always boasting that he ain't lost his old skills. He could be willing to ride out with you.'

'It's true I don't know much about Indians,' Greeley admitted. Usually he liked to ride on his own but for once he could be out of his depth. Having someone else along, who knew about Apaches, could mean the difference between success and failure. 'Where will I find him?'

'He usually hangs out in Walter's Bar.'

Greeley made a face. 'The last thing I need is the company or help of a drunkard.'

'Don't worry, he's not given to drinking much beyond a beer or two,' Hooper said. 'I agree with Eddie. He might at least be able to give you some idea about what to watch out for or where the Indians are likely to go. It's worth asking anyway.'

'I'll seek him out.'

'In the morning, Gus,' the doctor said sternly.

Greeley grinned and turned to Ann.

'Will you be all right on your own?'

'Oh no, I don't want to be by myself, not with Papa so bad.' She sounded afraid.

'Don't worry.' Hooper patted her hand. 'I'll get my wife to spend the night with you. Keep you company. And if there's any change in Sam's condition, she can send word to me and I'll come at once.'

Ann smiled her gratitude. 'Mr Greeley, you will be careful, won't you?'

'That I will.'

'And will I see you before you leave town tomorrow?'

'Yeah. I'll call in to find out how Sam is doing. I'm sure he'll be fine. I agree with the doc, he's too tough and too pig-headed for anything else.'

Ann smiled again and then flung her arms round him for a moment.

Thank you. Thank you for everything.'

'That's all right. Get some sleep. Things will look better in the morning. C'mon, Eddie, let's leave these good folks in peace.'

Now to get something to eat and then have that bath and haircut.

And enjoy a night at the brothel. He needed to see Melissa, hold her in his arms and go to sleep curled up next to her.

6

The Antlers was Elk Horn's largest saloon, occupying a corner plot in the middle of the red-light district. It had adobe walls, a wooden floor and glass in its windows. Behind the bar were mirrors interspersed with paintings of Western scenes. It was owned and run by Jack Phillips, a pugnacious man of forty. He was ugly with a bulbous nose, scar on his left cheek and thinning hair. His nature was ugly too. All he was interested in was making money by whatever means possible: mostly by letting others do the work for him as he was also incredibly lazy.

He generally employed two bartenders — they rarely stayed long because of his meanness — and a professional poker player; the present one didn't aim to hang around much longer either. It was said, although Greeley, who seldom played cards there, didn't know if it was true or not, that Phillips took a cut from every card game and didn't care whether the gambler was honest, or cheated in order to win. So long as he won was all that mattered.

A couple of girls also worked for him but they mainly just served drinks and talked to lonely cowboys because the brothel, run by Jack's sister, Josephine, was right next door.

Josephine was five years younger than Jack and couldn't exactly be called pretty. Her features were coarse and her hair lacklustre. Still, she treated the girls who worked for her quite well and neither exploited them nor allowed any of her customers to use violence, however much money they offered her.

The brothel was a swish affair with crimson drapes, red carpets and well-upholstered chairs. Paintings of richly endowed nudes were displayed on the walls. Josephine said it was the best place in the whole damn town and charged accordingly.

Greeley couldn't always afford to go there but tonight he could and so he did.

He woke up towards dawn with Melissa Fyfield nestled against him.

'Can't you sleep, hon?' she said in her Texan drawl.

'I keep thinking about Sam and those two Baker girls.'

'You did your best for the marshal and you didn't know about the girls.' Melissa stroked his cheek before getting out of bed, stark naked, and going over to the chest of drawers to pour each of them a whiskey. 'You couldn't've done more.'

Greeley sat up and leaned back against the pillows, staring at her in appreciation, considering her eye-achingly pretty. She was twenty-three with waist-length red hair, green-blue eyes and pink cheeks. She had an air of innocence about her that belied the fact that she'd been a prostitute for several years now.

Carrying the two glasses, she came back to the bed, sitting on the coverlet.

She clicked her glass with his.

'I reckon there ain't no easy way to say it but those girls could be in real trouble. Might even be better off dead. Did I ever tell you about my family?'

Greeley shook his head and grinned. When they were together there was usually little time for talk!

'Only that they were originally from South Carolina and they moved to Texas early on.'

'In 1821. Grandpappy, his two brothers, a sister and their families. They took up land right on the edge of civilization near where, in those days, the Comanches roamed wild and free and held sway over the whole area. The land was fertile and Grandpappy knew it would provide a good living for them all but it was very lonely and even more dangerous. He, like everyone else with any sense, feared the Indians. Luckily he was no fool.' Melissa smiled. 'He insisted the four families live close to one another and that they build a high stockade around the houses and the other buildings. And whenever anyone was out ploughing the fields or planting crops, two men went along as armed guards.'

'He was sensible.'

Melissa sipped her drink. 'He sure was. The Comanches, who only liked to fight when there was little risk to themselves, never bothered them. Never came near. A family a few miles up the creek wasn't so lucky.' Her face darkened. 'One day a band of Comanches attacked them just as it was getting dark. Grandpappy said the family were asking for trouble because they had stopped taking any precautions, had believed themselves safe because Indians hadn't been seen in the area for months, even though it was summer and the time of their hunting season. Even so, he said, no one deserved what happened to them.'

'What did happen?'

'Most of the men and all the older women were killed straight off. One man and several children, including a girl and boy both under the age of ten, were taken captive. As were two young women. Grandpappy led a posse after them.'

'Were they rescued?'

Melissa shivered. 'The first night out they heard a man screaming for hours on end until suddenly he stopped. The next day they found his badly tortured body. Near by was a girl of eighteen. Grandpappy never said what had been done to her but she was dead as well. The second white woman was in her twenties. She was married to a man who lived in the nearby town and was out visiting her sister, the dead girl, when the Comanches struck.'

She sighed at the woman's misfortune. 'Much later the tribe who held her captive traded her for supplies and she was returned to her husband.'

Greeley had the feeling that even so it wasn't going to be a happy ending. He was right.

'Her husband sent her back East to her family as he couldn't even look at her and wanted no more to do with her.

He said he couldn't bear the shame of what had been done to her. As if he was the one who'd been hurt. It's so unfair. It wasn't her fault. Scared and alone she had to suffer through whatever the Comanches did to her for months on end, and was then abandoned by her husband, who should have loved her and understood. Her family probably discarded her as well.' Another sigh. 'I often wonder what became of her.'

Greeley said nothing. As far as he was concerned the whole world was unfair but it was sometimes even more unfair to women. He'd never asked Melissa why a girl like her from a good family and with some education had become a prostitute; he couldn't imagine it would be out of choice. But now he thought that it was likely she'd been fooled and let down by some man and then her family had blamed her, said it was all her fault, and turned her out. It happened.

He took their glasses and put them on the table next to the bed. He pulled the girl close and held her to him, comforting her.

'I'll find the two Baker girls.' He made a promise both to Melissa and to himself.

'I know you'll do your best.'

Greeley reached up to hold her face and pull her down to kiss her.

It was quite some time later when Melissa, snuggled up against him, said, 'Have you heard the latest about Jack and Josephine?'

'No. What have that pair of scoundrels been up to now?'

'They want to give up their life here in Elk Horn and start up a ranch together.'

'What? Hell! Why on earth do they want to do that? Neither of them knows the first thing about ranching.'

'I know.' Melissa laughed. 'They reckon they're both getting too old for what they're doing and that it's hard work and becoming dangerous.'

'Hard work? Jack? He doesn't know the meaning of the words.'

'Dangerous anyway. Jack was almost shot a couple of weeks ago in a barroom brawl that got out of hand and Josephine has been threatened more'n once recently by drunken customers who don't want to pay what she charges. And, of course, they're always complaining that Marshal Detmeyer does nothing to protect them despite all the taxes they pay.'

Marshal Detmeyer, Greeley knew, didn't like either of the Phillips. But he was too honest to treat them other than fairly.

Stroking Melissa's hair, he said, 'With Apaches on the rampage, they might change their minds and think that staying in town is less dangerous than being out on a lonely ranch, where they'd be sitting targets. But supposing they do close down, what would you do?' He hoped she wouldn't move away.

'Oh, I reckon they'll be no shortage of people more'n willing to run both the saloon and the brothel.' She bit her lip. 'They might not run it as well as Josephine or be so nice to us girls though.'

Greeley didn't answer because there was little he could say. He knew as well as she did that the life of a prostitute was full of risks. Men sometimes paid for them not for pleasure but to inflict pain.

7

Walter's Bar was a small and dirty saloon at the far end of the red-light district, catering to the rowdy or those with not much money.

When Greeley got there early the next morning the place was empty except for a whiskery drunk sleeping it off in a corner and snoring loudly, and another man who was sitting at a table drinking coffee and eating a plate of bacon and beans. He looked up as Greeley came in but otherwise took no notice of him. Nor did the half-asleep bartender who was wiping down the bar.

Greeley hoped the drunk wasn't the scout he sought but rather thought it must be the other man. He certainly looked the part. He was about sixty with greying hair, straggling down to his shoulders, and sharp dark eyes. His face was brown and leathery. Wearing jeans and a shirt, he had on a vest decorated with conch shells and beads and was wearing beaded moccasins. A Bowie knife was stuck in the belt of his trousers.

'Are you Mr Henry Walsh?' Greeley stopped a little way from the table.

'Who wants to know?'

'My name's Gustavus Greeley . . . '

'Oh yeah, you're that bounty hunter, ain't you?' The man regarded him. 'Successful too so I hear. How can I help you? Sit down. Hey, Walter, bring us both some coffee.'

Quickly Greeley told Walsh what had happened the day before. The man listened without speaking and Greeley had the feeling he didn't believe him.

'And two young girls are missing, you say?'

'That's right.'

'So, what d'you want from me?'

'You're good at following a trail . . . '

'You must be too to follow and find wanted outlaws for a living. I guess they don't always make it easy for you.'

'Some of them don't for sure. But you used to be an army scout. You know Indians and their ways. I don't. Will you come with me out to the farm? At least show me what I should be looking for. Point me in the right direction.'

From the way the scout was behaving, Greeley doubted he would agree. So he was quite surprised when Walsh nodded and said:

'Yeah, OK.' He drank the last of his coffee. 'I'd sure like to see this Indian raid for myself. When you going?'

'Soon. I've just got one or two things to do first.'

'I'll go on down to the livery. Meet you there.'

'Thanks.'

'Don't thank me just yet,' Walsh said, making Greeley wonder what he meant.

Gus next went to the marshal's office where Eddie Smith was busy arranging breakfast for the drunken prisoners he had locked up in the cells.

'Have you been to see how Marshal Detmeyer is this morning?' Greeley asked.

Eddie shook his head. 'With all that's happening here,' a nod indicated the cells, 'I haven't had the time or opportunity.'

'All right, I'll go there in a minute. Any other news?'

'Nothing about the telegraph, no. But, Mr Greeley, two young cowboys from the CW Circle ranch came in last night round about midnight. They were shit scared. They'd been attacked by Apaches and one of 'em had an arrow wound in his leg.'

'Where did the attack take place?'

'Somewhere over at the end of Five-Mile Valley. Where the CW Circle land begins.'

'Where are the cowboys now? Have they gone back to the ranch?'

'I doubt it. Not with the state they were in. They're likely lying drunk some place.'

'OK. If they're still in town when I get back later on I'll hear for myself what

56

they have to say.' Greeley frowned. 'The Indians must've decided the valley would give them rich pickings. I just hope there aren't any more folks living that way who've been raided.'

'Same here.'

'I'll be busy trying to find the Baker girls. But perhaps you can round up a few men to ride out and make sure no one else is hurt and also that the farmers over that way are warned about what's going on.'

'Yeah, OK.'

Greeley got to the door, then turned back.

'By the way, Eddie, can you get someone to go out to the Baker's farm sometime today and deal with the livestock. There are a couple of horses out there and a milk cow. Make sure they don't go alone, just in case the Indians are still around.'

'Sure thing, Mr Greeley. OK, OK, breakfast's coming!' he added in a yell as his prisoners started clamouring for food.

It was the doctor's wife, Kathryn,

who answered the door of the marshal's house. She was a short, plump woman who helped her husband with such patients as pregnant mothers and sick children. She smiled when she saw Greeley, so he knew that the news, while it might not be good, wasn't bad either.

'There's no change in Sam's condition,' she said. 'Bradley's been by to look at him and he says that Sam is holding his own.'

'That's good. How's Ann?'

'Bradley gave her something to help her sleep. And she's still in bed. Don't worry, Gus, I'll stay here with her. I'll make sure she's not left alone. And, Gus, I surely do hope you have luck in finding those two girls. I just hate to think how frightened and alone they must be.'

8

Keeping his word, Walsh was at the livery stable when Greeley got there. He'd saddled his pinto mare and also Greeley's own horse, a black gelding with a white nose, so they were ready to leave straight away.

'Were you a scout for a long time, Mr Walsh?' Greeley said, making conversation as they started along the trail to the Baker farm. He liked to know something about whoever he was with.

'Sure was, son.' A faraway look came into the old man's eyes. 'I came out West when I was a youngster. I think I was just fourteen but I ain't too sure as I ain't too sure when I was exactly born. Couldn't stand the crowded East. All those folks pressing in on me. Pa expecting me to follow him into the family business. He was a baker of all damn things, working long hours of the day and night for little reward and much criticism.

'At first I roamed around some on my own, working for fur trappers an' such and learning my trade. Before long, though, I signed up for the army. Rode with Kit Carson a time or two. Travelled all over the south-west: Arizona, New Mexico, Utah. Even up into Colorado. Across to California once. Now that was a place for sure! Never was so foolish as to search for gold though. It was a good life. Dangerous sure. Got wounded several times. But free and wild.'

'What made you give up?'

'Got too old.' Walsh frowned. 'And after the Civil War ended things changed quickly. People started to come out here. More and more stagecoach' routes. Then the damn railroad arrived. Hell, everything got too damn civilized. Couldn't hardly ride a mile or two without coming to a town or a ranch with its damned barbed wire. Even worse was when the farmers moved in with their conventional way of life, expecting everyone to be the same, and follow the same rules. Whole place is going to hell. Hell, I'm thinking of moving on while there's still some wild country to move on to.' Walsh spat out a wad of chewing tobacco.

'Where would that be?'

'Up in Wyoming or Montana maybe. Only trouble is it's damn cold up in those parts in the winter and my bones feel the cold these days. Another thing — there ain't hardly no Indians around now that ain't living out their days on reservations. Poor bastards. Dying of boredom most like and existing on putrid meat handed out to them by the corrupt government.' Another hawk and a spit.

'Well, it seems like some have broken out of the Reservation now.'

'We'll see.'

Again Greeley wondered what the scout meant, but when he asked Walsh simply shrugged as if he wouldn't be believed. So Greeley changed the subject.

'Have you family?'

'Not no more. Was once married to a

Navajo squaw. Pretty little thing she was. Gave me two boys. But when she upped and died and I upped and left, I left 'em with the tribe. Hell, son, don't look at me like that. I ain't never really fitted in with the white man's world, so how could they? They were better off where they were. Had a few years living the old ways anyway. Ain't seen 'em since.'

'Why did you leave the tribe?'

'Nothing there for me without her. And while I ain't keen on white man's civilization I ain't an Indian and I don't belong in their world either.' Walsh sighed. 'What about you, son? You married?'

'Not yet.' Greeley thought that if his dreams of becoming a farmer had come true, he would by now have a wife and children of his own. He didn't say so to Walsh, seeing how the scout felt about farmers.

They fell silent then and it wasn't until they approached the farm that Walsh spoke again.

'You say there were three dead 'uns up there?'

'Yeah.'

'First thing then you'd better bury 'em.'

'Shouldn't we start after the Indians?' That was uppermost in Greeley's mind.

'Bodies need burying. Tell you what.' Walsh grinned wickedly. 'You're so anxious to get on the trail, you can do all the digging while I do the searching around.'

Greeley was quickly coming to wonder whether having Henry Walsh along was a good idea. He was used to working by himself, doing what he wanted and when. Now it seemed the scout was calling the shots. However, when they reached the house he decided Walsh was right. Several buzzards were circling the sky and when he opened the door, an overpowering smell of decay almost made him gag. There were more flies than before, too, hovering like black clouds over each of the bodies.

He closed the door quickly and went to find the best place to bury the three people. In the meantime Walsh was walking about the yard, studying the ground.

'You notice this?' He beckoned Greeley to his side.

'What is it?'

'Spatters of blood. Reckon one of the raiders was shot.'

'Good.' Greeley hoped the man was hurt real bad. 'It should make it easier for us to track them.'

Leaving Walsh to it, he found a patch of land just beyond the burnt-out barn where the earth was fairly easy to dig. He found a spade in one of the work buildings, took off his jacket and began to dig three graves, gathering up rocks and stones to pile on top of the earth so that no bird or animal could reach the bodies. He decided that as soon as he got back to town he'd order the undertaker to make three crosses. It didn't seem right not to leave a marker of some sort.

With Walsh's help, he carried the bodies out to the graves and laid them down. He said a prayer over them and Walsh said some Navajo words afterwards.

It was hot and dusty work and by the time he'd done, Greeley was irritable, sweaty and his arms ached. He went back to his horse and had a long pull at the canteen.

'Have you found a trail?' he asked, wiping his forehead free of sweat.

'Sure have.'

'Let's go then.'

'Hold up a minute, son. I've got something to say and you might not like it.'

'You're not going with me?'

'Yeah, I am. So you don't go more wrong in your thinking than you already have.'

'What do you mean?'

'Listen. You need to know this before we start out.'

Greeley was puzzled, wondering what the man was going to say.

'You still reckon it was Apaches done this?'

'Of course.' Greeley was surprised. 'Who else?'

'Well, son, it surely don't look that way to me. I don't think Apaches, or any type of Indian come to that, were responsible.'

9

'What the hell!' Greeley said, adding angrily, 'Of course it was Apaches! God-dammit the Bakers were shot through with arrows.'

'Oh, I agree it looks like Apaches raided here. But, hell, son, it's all wrong.'

'No, it ain't. In what way could all this . . . ' Greeley waved a hand around the farmyard, 'be wrong? And what about those two cowboys? They were attacked too. They're witnesses, god-dammit!'

'Gus, you asked for my help because I was an army scout for years, hunting Indians, following their tracks and learning their ways. Hell, I lived with them for a long time. I know them and their ways. Don't go ignoring me or saying I'm old and stupid and don't know what I'm talking about just because you don't like what I'm telling you.'

Greeley reddened a little. He had been thinking Walsh must be past his prime to be spouting what he considered nonsense.

'Hear me out.'

'OK Why don't you think Indians did this?' Greeley's tone was sarcastic. 'Convince me if you can.'

'Well, for a start there ain't been any trouble in these parts for several years now, even before the Apaches were herded on to the Reservation by the damn government. And the Reservation is run pretty well, all things considered, and the land is good for crops. Why risk it being taken away? Risk being sent to Florida where the conditions would make it like living in a hell hole?'

'Apaches don't like being forced to be farmers. They prefer to be out hunting.'

'Granted, but they ain't foolish, although some white folks think they are. They know those days are long

68

gone. They know there ain't much to hunt around here any more, or open land on which to ride.'

'That might be all right for the elders of the tribe, they might've accepted that, but not necessarily the young bucks who'd like to recapture the spirit of the old days they've heard so much about. And you can't deny that not so long ago Indians often broke out of their Reservations to raid ranches of cattle an' such. Still do, so I've heard.'

Walsh spread his hands. 'That was mostly in places where the government broke the treaties and provided the Indians with bad meat or no meat at all. Broke other promises too, or instigated a harsh regime with punishments for every little infringement. That ain't the case here. Cap'n Harding at Fort Myerson runs things fairly. He's firm but reasonable.'

'Even so . . . '

'And, Gus, more than that, take a look around you. There's been no destruction of the house or buildings

— apart from the barn, that is,' Walsh quickly added as Greeley opened his mouth to object. 'And no desecration of the bodies. Believe me, I doubt very much whether any Indian out for a good time and with his blood lust up would, after killing three people, leave 'em behind without scalping 'em or otherwise mutilating their bodies. It wouldn't be in their nature.'

'They might've been disturbed by Marshal Detmeyer riding in.'

'Detmeyer was shot. He wasn't a threat to anyone. They could've taken the time to scalp him too. And these days I doubt they'd ride away with captives.'

'Not even two young girls?'

'No. In the old days when they could disappear into the wilderness, yes. But these days, like I said, there ain't much wilderness left. No, if they wanted to violate those girls they'd've done it here and killed them as well.'

Greeley was angry that Walsh could speak so unemotionally about such things when the very thought of them made him all the more furious.

'They could've been taken as hostages. In case the Indians needed something to bargain with for their freedom.'

'Mebbe.' Walsh shook his head. 'But that don't seem right either. Bucks come off the Reservation to raid; they'd hope to slip back on to the Reservation without anyone being any the wiser and so they'd have no need for hostages.'

'The Indians who attacked the Bakers could have decided to run for Mexico. Plenty of Apaches have done just that and hidden out in the Chiricahuas.'

'Then they're heading in the wrong direction.'

'You've got an answer for everything.' Greeley was getting angrier by the minute. 'Sounds to me like you've always been on the side of the Indians and still are.' His hands clenched into fists.

'No I ain't, although I've always been

able to see their side as well as the white man's. But believe me none of this is right. Look here, there are five separate tracks of horses in the yard, besides those that the marshal and you rode in on and they was all shod. Indians don't ride shod horses. And while four of 'em were ridden out up the valley, the fifth went off in the opposite direction to the others. Back towards Elk Horn. Why would an Indian go there?'

Despite himself, Greeley was impressed. He considered himself a pretty good tracker but he couldn't have picked out so much detail, not with the way the yard was churned up. He pushed his hat to the back of his head and rubbed his forehead. He didn't know what to think or believe.

'So if you're right, and I ain't saying you are, someone has gone to an awful lot of trouble and an awful lot of killing to make all this look like an Apache raid. Why? Who would do that? And why the Bakers?'

'First off, perhaps the Bakers upset

someone real bad and made themselves an enemy.'

'OK, yeah, I guess. But that doesn't explain why the two cowboys were attacked or why anyone would go to the bother of dressing it up like this.'

'White folks are always trying to stir up trouble for Indians. Always have and always will.'

Greeley knew that only too well but he still said, 'Why?', as if he didn't.

'Mostly because they don't like people who are different to them with different ideas and different ways. They like everything to be civilized. Or because they're greedy or resentful of even the little left to the Indians.' Walsh shrugged. 'Indians have always been handed a raw deal and I can't see it getting any better. Not any time soon.'

'You should remember that three innocent people have been killed here, one a woman and another a boy. And two girls are missing. You should think of them and Marshal Detmeyer first, not the bloodthirsty bastards who caused the outrage.'

'That's what I am doing. And I'm trying to get you to see sense, too. Believe me, son, there's been killings on both sides with white men causing many an outrage against the red.'

There was no reasoning with the man. He was unreasonable. But Greeley still needed him. So he swallowed his temper as best he could and said: 'Are you going to help me find whoever did this? Whoever it was?'

Walsh grinned. 'Sure am, just so I can prove I'm right.'

'Let's get going then. Should be easy to track four riders, especially if one of the bastards is hurt.'

Unfortunately it didn't work out like that.

* * *

It was the middle of the morning when Ann Detmeyer eventually woke up. She usually got up early, never later than seven o'clock, and for a moment she

74

couldn't imagine why she was still in bed when the sun was shining brightly outside and sending warm rays across the room.

Then she remembered.

Her father was hurt. Had been shot — with an arrow!

Quickly she got out of bed and pulled a wrap around her. As she went into the hallway the door to her father's room opened and Mrs Hooper emerged.

'I thought I heard you getting up,' she said.

'How is Papa?'

'He's all right, dear,' Mrs Hooper said, taking hold of her hands. 'He's had a good night and is sleeping peacefully at the moment. The doctor has been by and he's more than pleased. There's no sign of infection or fever. Doctor thinks your father is past the critical stage and so long as he's kept warm and comfortable and the wound is kept clean he should be fine.'

'Oh thank goodness.' Ann felt quite weak at the knees.

'Why don't you sit beside him while I make you something to eat?'

'Oh no. I couldn't eat a thing.'

'Some coffee then and maybe a couple of eggs. I'll scramble them. And perhaps add some beans. You'll feel better then.'

Ann didn't argue.

Her father being hurt was something she'd always dreaded. He was a good lawman, normally well able to look after himself, and well respected in the town of Elk Horn. But there was always the chance that some drunken or wild young man would decide to go up against him. Would be fast on the draw and faster on the trigger. Or that her father would be hurt during a robbery or trouble at one of the saloons.

But this? To be shot by Apaches? It seemed impossible.

Tears came into Ann's eyes and she wiped them away. Crying would do no good. But her father was all she had. Her mother had died ten years ago and to her shame Ann could barely remember her. There were no brothers or sisters, except for two babies buried in graves in the town cemetery. After that it had been her and her father, together, against the world. It would always be like that even when Ann went on to have a husband and children of her own.

He had to be all right. Had to be. He would be.

At least she knew she could depend on Mr Greeley. He would avenge the deaths of the Bakers. He would find Claire and Rachel and rescue them too. She had every faith in Gus. He was a good man.

10

'Look, Gus,' Walsh said as they rode out of the yard, 'two of the horses have left much deeper impressions than the other two. I figure they're carrying two riders.'

Greeley could see that for himself.

'The girls,' he stated.

'Gotta be. And there, that's a spot of blood. Idiots. You'd think they'd've had the sense to bind up the wound so it wouldn't bleed. Don't reckon he was hit bad though. Ain't enough blood for that.'

'Pity. I'd like to think of the bastard suffering.'

'They're heading up Five-Mile Valley.'

'Yeah, to where they attacked the cowboys.'

'You wanna go see where that happened?'

'No, there's no real point. I'd rather

follow the trail and rescue the girls.'

'Anyway it would be stupid to continue much further up the valley. That way they'd come to a helluva lot of ranches and farms. I remember when it was open land and you could ride all day without seeing anyone or anything.'

'Where d'you think they'll go?' Greeley interrupted the old man's reminiscences.

'I reckon they'll turn off and ride into the foothills. It's still mostly empty country up there. Just trees and rocks criss-crossed with the odd narrow, twisting trail. A few meadows where ranchers graze cattle. And the odd line shack. That's all.'

Greeley nodded. He'd been up in the hills a time or two. They were lonely and quiet, silent mostly. He'd never seen anyone there.

'It won't be easy to track 'em,' Walsh said.

He was right.

They were soon riding uphill, and once amongst the trees it wasn't long before they reached the stream that eventually emptied out into the river serving Elk Horn. It was shallow and meandered between low banks, shaded by sycamores and pine trees, with wooded hills stretching away on both sides.

The raiders had ridden into the water and it was there that Greeley and Walsh lost their tracks and their trail. They hadn't simply crossed the stream and come out on its far side, they had stayed in the water.

'Find anything?' Greeley asked when Walsh rode back from searching downstream.

'Nope.'

'Me neither.' Greeley felt dispirited. It had been going well. He'd believed they would find the killers, whoever they were, before long. Now . . . ?

Walsh shook his head. 'They could have gone for miles in either direction. It'll take us too long to find out which. Our best bet is to stop looking.'

'Hey, now!'

'Sorry, Gus, it's hopeless.'

Greeley clamped down on his anger. Walsh was meant to have been an army scout. For years. Yet he seemed to have lost the trail all too easily, and didn't seem any too anxious to find it again. Was that because he was so old now as not to be as good as he'd once been? That wasn't likely, as he'd spotted things Greeley had missed; or was he saying it was hopeless on purpose because he didn't want his damn pals, the Apaches, to be found and caught? Wanted them to escape or return to the Reservation and pretend they'd never left?

'We can't just give up.'

'Ain't saying we should.'

'What then?'

'We can ride to Fort Myerson.'

'But that's some two hours' ride in the other direction. Taking us away from where the raiders and the Baker girls are. Besides, what would we do there?'

'There, son, we can make enquiries

81

as to whether or not there has been a breakout so we'll know whether we're searching for Apaches or white men. Iffen I'm wrong and it should happen to be Indians, we can ask for the army's help in tracing 'em. Cap'n Harding can send men out to fix the telegraph lines and while they're at it they can do a bit of searching for tracks as well. C'mon, Gus, riding up and down the river here is a waste of our time.'

Reluctantly Greeley had to admit the old man was right.

* * *

The Antlers saloon was usually quiet on a Sunday morning, when the townsmen were spending time with their families and attending church, and the cowboys, with hangovers and drunken memories, were riding back to their ranches. The brothel closed its doors every morning too, thus allowing the girls to get some much needed rest.

Jack Phillips spent the time going

over his accounts; he was usually joined by Josephine counting out her Saturday-night takings.

'Good night last night,' Josephine said with a greedy smile as she put the money into a velvet bag. 'Lots to take to the bank. What about you?'

'Not bad.'

Josephine smiled again. She knew that meant her brother had done as well as she had, perhaps even better. He was never one to say he was pleased or happy about anything.

'I reckon it means we'll soon have enough to start looking for land, don't you?'

Phillips rubbed his nose. 'Yeah. Any day now. Only trouble is most of the really good land around here has already been taken up.'

That was a common refrain; amongst others as well as Jack.

'There's good land over on that damn Reservation. You said so yourself.'

'I know. And I reckon if the damn Apaches continue with their raiding they'll be in real trouble and the land will be taken away from 'em, which is no more'n they deserve.'

Brother and sister grinned at one another.

'Be cheap too, I shouldn't wonder.'

'I can't wait to quit this life,' Josephine said with a sigh. 'I'm getting too old for it. We're going to do it this time, ain't we, Jack, like we planned and you promised?'

'Sure . . .' Phillips began, then broke off to moan, 'Oh hell, here comes a customer.' Not trusting anyone, he quickly hid the takings under the bar.

'It's that newcomer to town. David Preston his name is.' Josephine stood up a little straighter and patted her hair to make sure it was tidy. She very seldom went with any of the brothel's customers these days but that didn't mean she wasn't attracted to a handsome man.

Preston *was* handsome. He was nearing thirty, tall and broad-shouldered, with dark-brown hair that reached almost to his shoulders, and a bushy brown

84

beard. He had a pleasant face. Even better, he had plenty of money if his store-bought suit and shoes were anything to go by. So far he hadn't visited the brothel, although his younger brother, Will, had on several occasions. David looked the gentleman but Will had a wild streak. They were originally from Kansas.

'What can I get you?' Phillips asked.

'Beer, please.' Preston put some coins down on the counter. 'Buy you two a drink as well?' Neither Jack nor Josephine said no. 'I was wondering if you knew how Marshal Detmeyer was doing. It was a terrible thing that happened to him and to those folks up at the farm.'

Phillips didn't have a great deal of time for the law but grudgingly he supposed that Detmeyer was better than some and for a small monthly fee he allowed both saloon and brothel to operate without much interference. He wasn't surprised that Preston had come here to learn what was going on. The Antlers was a hotbed of gossip.

'Hear tell that Detmeyer is still unconscious. But Doc Hooper is hopeful he'll
pull through,' Phillips replied.

'That's good news. Me and my
brother have rented rooms in a house
just down the street from the marshal
and his daughter. She seems a nice girl
and will surely be devastated if anything
bad happened to her father.'

'Sure would,' Josephine said, not that
she knew much about nice girls and
didn't have time for them either.

'Damn Indians.'

'Me and Josephine feel the same. Think
they can do anything they like and then
run back to the Reservation and the
army will protect 'em. Probably will too.
It ain't right. It ain't fair. People out
here work hard for what they've got and
they're the ones need protecting. Don't
happen though.'

Preston nodded solemnly and drank
some of his beer.

'As you may know, my brother and
me have come out here to buy land.
Start up a ranch.'

'What we want to do too,' Josephine said.

'Really? But quite frankly this has made us think again. We thought from all we'd read that this area would be safe and ideal for us. Now what with these attacks and the fact that the Apaches are sitting on the best land still available we're not so sure.'

'Just what we were saying and there are plenty of people in Elk Horn feel the same as us,' Josephine said. 'They'll be real angry about all that's happened.'

'I shouldn't worry too much, Mr Preston.' Phillips smiled. 'I reckon the problem will soon be sorted out, and the Apaches put in their rightful place. Which as far as I'm concerned is as far from here as possible.'

'You think so?'

'Surely do.'

'That's good because we both like it here and wouldn't really want to go elsewhere.'

'Doubt it'll come to that.'

11

'There she is,' Walsh said. He brought his horse to a halt and pointed. 'Fort Myerson.'

The fort was situated in the middle of a vast and otherwise empty meadow that formed part of the Reservation, although there was no sign here of any Indians or their dwelling places. It was fertile land, being near to a river, green and lush even at this time of the year: ideal for both growing crops and keeping cattle.

The fort itself was quite large. While it wasn't surrounded by a stockade, there was a tall watchtower and the buildings were arranged so that they formed their own defensive walls. Nearby was a long, low trading post made of adobe, for the Apaches, as well as a saloon, strictly for the soldiers.

As they rode closer Greeley could see

quite a lot of activity going on. Several infantrymen, recruits by the looks of them, were being put through their paces on the parade ground, bawled at by a hefty sergeant, his shouts getting louder each time they did something wrong. Ten or so cavalrymen were trotting their horses across the meadow. A couple of officers crossed from one building to the next.

When they dismounted outside the post headquarters the door opened immediately and a man wearing a captain's uniform came out. He was in his forties, a weather-beaten man with a capable air.

'Henry! Thought it was you,' he said with a broad smile. 'Good to see you again.'

'Cap'n.' Walsh gave a sketchy salute in reply. He slipped off his horse. Greeley did likewise and Walsh introduced him. 'This is Captain James Harding, Gus, the fort's commanding officer.'

They shook hands.

'It's not often you come here these days, Henry. What can I do for you?'

'Got some news. Bad too.'

Harding frowned. 'Best come in then. Sergeant Kendall,' he added in a roar and a young man came running from the direction of the forge. 'Sergeant, see to these gentlemen's horses. You hungry?' he asked Walsh.

'And thirsty,' Walsh replied. 'We've had a long and hot ride.'

'Get someone to serve beer and slices of beef with some crackers.'

Harding then turned on his heel and led the way inside, where it was blessedly cool after the heat of the early afternoon. He took them into his office and, sitting behind his paper-strewn desk, indicated that they should sit down opposite him.

'All right, Henry, what's this all about?'

Walsh nodded to Greeley, who said, 'Yesterday afternoon in Five-Mile Valley a farmer and his family was attacked and killed. They were shot through with arrows.'

'What?' Harding sat up straight.

Quickly Greeley told the captain all

that he'd found at the Bakers' farm and how two girls were missing, taken captive. Harding turned to the ex-scout.

'What do you make of it, Henry?'

'Like I done told Gus, I don't think Apaches were responsible but someone has sure gone to a lot of trouble to make it appear as if they were. They also cut the telegraph lines.'

'But you think it is Indians, don't you?' Harding said to Greeley.

'At first sight it sure looks that way to me.'

'And if you do, so will a lot of other white folks. I don't like this.'

Greeley sat forward. 'So, Captain, what I want to know is whether or not you've had any Indians causing trouble on the Reservation, or whether you know of any who've left in the last few days to go out on raids and who are perhaps still out?'

Harding steepled his hands under his chin. 'I can honestly say, Mr Greeley, that the answer is no, at least as far as I'm aware. There has been nothing going on recently, no whispers of any kind. Everything is real peaceful at the moment and has been for a long while.'

He must have seen the scepticism on Greeley's face as he went on, 'Oh, don't get me wrong, you have the young bucks making noises now and then, which is only natural, and I'm not saying that some of them don't slip out on rustling raids on occasion, but nothing like this. The murder of an innocent family. Why would they do that and put in jeopardy everything they have here?'

Walsh glanced at Greeley and nodded. 'Just what I said.'

'The tribal elders mostly keep the young and the wild under control and tell them in no uncertain terms, as do I, that if they cause too much trouble the whole tribe will be punished, with their privileges being taken away. No one would risk that.'

Walsh nodded, although Greeley still wasn't entirely convinced. He said, 'They get stirred up enough they might not take the risks into account.'

'As far as I know there's been nothing

remotely like trouble in quite a while.'

'You know that for sure?'

'Mr Greeley, I take this job extremely seriously. I send men out on regular patrols both through the Reservation and into the surrounding countryside to make sure everything is all right. I also have regular meetings with the tribal elders. So I'd certainly hope I would know if something was wrong. Ah, good, here's the food. Help yourselves.'

Greeley poured himself a glass of beer and drank half of it down in one swallow. It was cold and bitter, just how he liked it. He was also hungry and the thick slices of beef looked tasty.

'Could Indians have come into the area from elsewhere?'

'I doubt it. As I said, my men patrol regularly and they certainly haven't reported anything like that to me.'

'OK, I can see you agree with Henry.' Greeley tried not to show his anger and frustration. 'But if the Apaches aren't responsible then who is? More impor-tant: why try to make it *look* like

Indians on a raid?'

'White men are always trying to get the Indians blamed for everything.'

'So you've said, Henry!' Greeley snapped. 'There must be something more to it than that.'

Harding poured out more beer for them all. 'Unfortunately, Henry is right. White men and Indians don't usually mix too well, even these days, and of course there are faults on both sides. As for a reason, well look around you, Mr Greeley, what do you see? This Reservation is on prime farming land.'

Greeley nodded.

'There was uproar when the Apaches were first granted it ... ' Harding continued.

'Despite it being part of their tribal lands,' Walsh put in.

' ... and every now and then someone gets up and starts shouting the odds about why should the dastardly and treacherous Indian have so much good land, when they don't farm it properly, which isn't true, and have no real use for it,

94

which isn't true either, when there are decent white folks going without.'

Captain Harding sounded as much on the side of the Indians as Walsh. At the same time Greeley had read those sorts of reports in the newspapers and knew that what Harding said was true. He wondered why folks, whatever their colour, couldn't just get along, especially when there was surely enough land for everyone.

'So you think this could be a ploy to say: oh well, the Indians are up to their old tricks again, and get the government to take the Reservation away from them?'

'And put them on piss-poor land where nothing grows,' Walsh said. 'Happened before, will doubtless happen again.'

Harding gave his ex-scout a little smile. 'I don't know for certain if that is the case here, but sadly it seems all too likely. It would be a real shame, a travesty of justice, if the Apaches had their land taken away from them when they've worked so hard to farm it.'

'Especially for something they ain't done.'

Although Greeley was reluctant, and didn't want to admit it, he was starting to come round to the other two men's way of thinking. They knew Apaches and how they behaved. Why would they lie just to protect them?

He said, 'What I don't understand is, if you're right, and I'm not yet saying you are, where did the men get the bows and arrows from?'

Walsh laughed. 'Doubt that'd be difficult. Might've bought 'em some place or stole 'em from a bunch of Indians they attacked at some time.'

'Not recently,' Harding said with a frown. 'Not round here anyway. I would have been told if any of my Apaches had been robbed. No, more likely they bought them some place. What about from Archie Ford?'

'Who's that?' Greeley asked. Harding turned to him.

'He trades with the Indians all over this area. Has done for years. Used to sell them obsolete guns in return for turquoise jewellery and other artefacts, which are collected by those in the East. These days, with the Indians no longer on the warpath and needing guns, he trades in anything that can be bought and sold for a profit.'

'Supplied 'em with rotgut whiskey too, I heard,' Walsh added. 'And still does.'

'So I believe. I'm sure he keeps a ready supply of bows and arrows. He certainly used to.'

'He still around?'

Harding shrugged. 'You know Ford, Henry; no sooner is he shut down some-where so he starts up some place else. Last I heard he had what he grandly called a trading post a few miles from here, tucked away down Elk Canyon.'

'I know the place,' Walsh said. 'We can visit there on our way back to town, Gus. It's not far. See what Archie has to say.'

'OK. The sooner we get to the bottom of this the better.'

'In the meantime I'll send some men

out to repair the telegraph lines and to warn people on some of the isolated farms and ranches nearby to be on their guard. And, Mr Greeley, if Apaches should happen to be responsible, then I can do something about that too. Otherwise . . . ' Harding shrugged. It wouldn't be his problem then. 'I'll also go right now and speak to the tribal leaders myself. Warn them too.' He shook his head. 'But, like Henry, I don't think anyone on the Reservation has done this.'

'You know, Captain, there's nothing to be done for the Bakers now but I'm real concerned about those two girls.'

Harding frowned and glanced at Walsh. 'I'm afraid to say it's likely they're already dead. But that doesn't mean we shouldn't search for them and find their bodies. Give them a decent burial.'

'I hope you're wrong.'

'So do I.'

But Greeley could tell that Captain Harding was certain he was right.

12

'What's happening?' Rachel Baker asked in a frightened voice.

From outside the tiny, smelly hut where she and Claire were being held captive came the sound of a drunken roar.

'I'm scared.'

'Hush, I'll go and see,' Claire said.

She and Rachel were sitting at the rear of the hut, arms around one another for comfort and protection. Now Claire let her sister go and stood up, tiptoeing over to the hut's one window. It was covered with a piece of sacking but there was a slit at the bottom, allowing her to peer out without attracting the attention of their captors.

'They're getting drunk,' she said in a whisper over her shoulder. 'Again.'

There were four of them. The hateful, horrible men, who had attacked the farm and killed their parents and Frank. A fifth man had been with them but he'd ridden away in the direction of Elk Horn. Now there they sat, sprawled round a dying campfire, passing a bottle of whiskey to and fro between them, and laughing. Laughing! How dare they! It was as if they weren't in the least bit concerned about what they'd done. Had enjoyed the killing and the terror. The deaths meant nothing to them.

The two girls were not only completely distraught over what had happened to their family but petrified at what was going to happen to them. But Claire was also mad with anger. She wanted nothing more than to punish these men. If the chance came she would kill them with no qualms whatsoever. Her eyes glittered with furious tears. What they had done was monstrous and she would never ever forgive them.

The attack had come out of nowhere in the early afternoon. Their father and Frank had just been leaving to finish working in one of the fields and she and

Rachel were going to help their mother put away the fresh laundry. Over their midday meal they'd been discussing the proposed trip into town at the beginning of next week, looking forward to the chance for some shopping and catching up with friends. Then everything fell apart.

One minute life on the farm was the same as usual, busy, quiet and peaceful, the next the air was full of Indian war-whoops and the barn was alight.

It had quickly become obvious that Indians weren't responsible for the attack. Five white men were riding about in the yard, firing arrows at the house.

Their father had ordered Claire and Rachel to hide in the root cellar, although both had wanted to stay and fight. Their mother refused to go with them. Frank had shot and hit one of the raiders, crying out with delight as he did so.

But it was hopeless. They were up against five ruthless men and the Bakers were farmers, not fighters. Between them they had one rifle, which was used for shooting vermin, two revolvers and not much in the way of ammunition. They'd never needed more.

The end was inevitable, prolonged only because the raiders were enjoying themselves, frightening the folks in the house. They could be heard urging one another on, joking as they did so.

Then as the girls clutched one another in the cellar they heard shouting, a door crashing open. Their mother's screams, which stopped abruptly. One yell from their father, another frightened one from Frank.

All at once everything fell silent. That was until the attackers began to crash about in the room above the cellar, knocking things over and smashing crockery as they tramped from room to room.

For a little while the girls thought they might be safe, that the men wouldn't find them. No such luck. Suddenly the trapdoor was flung open and two men looked down on them. Maybe they had hoped to find food but, laughing, calling out to their friends, it was obvious they thought they'd found something much more to their taste.

As the girls were dragged up and out they'd seen their parents and brother lying dead. But the men didn't let the girls go to them. They were hustled outside. Rachel had started crying but Claire clenched her fists so tight they hurt, and bit her lip, refusing to let these men know how distressed and frightened she was. In the yard they'd been kept under guard by one of the men while the others continued to loot the house. Eventually the men had come out of the house.

'What shall we do with these two?' the youngest of them said.

'Let's take 'em with us,' another said. 'That's what real Injuns would do.'

Struggling and screaming, the girls were flung up on two of the horses and the men mounted behind them, holding them so tightly that escape was impossible.

At the very same moment Marshal Detmeyer had ridden up and dismounted in front of the house. Hearing their cries he'd come running round the side of the house, gun out ready.

'Watch out!' Claire had called.

But her warning was too late. He'd been shot in the back by the fifth raider, who had kept to the shadows of the barn. He was the one who hadn't accompanied the others to the hut but had ridden away, saying he'd see them all later. They'd all laughed about the marshal being shot.

'Serve him right,' one man said and kicked Detmeyer's body.

'Let him bleed to death and let's get outta here!'

Then they'd spurred their horses into a gallop, whooping some more, as they rode out of the yard.

It had taken them quite a while to reach this hut, the men's hideout, as once they were in the foothills, they'd taken great care to hide their tracks.

'Just like the boss told us to,' one of them said, sounding proud that he'd remembered. Claire thought his name was Nate. He was the one who'd kicked Detmeyer.

They'd spent a great deal of time splashing through the river and had come out where the ground was stony and hard.

Once at their destination the girls were shut inside the hut.

Later on Nate and one of the others had ridden away and Claire thought that maybe this was their chance to escape. But the two who remained behind had sat on guard outside the hut, alert enough to be able to stop any such attempt. It hadn't been long before the other two men returned. From their boasting it sounded like they'd staged another so-called raid. This time on a couple of cowboys.

'Shit scared,' Nate said, making the others laugh.

'This'll sure make people round here sit up and take notice,' said someone else.

All four had then promptly proceeded to get drunk. The youngest one had remembered the captives enough to bring them some water to drink and some horrible-looking and worse-tasting stew to eat. Otherwise they'd been left alone. Perhaps that was because the men were soon in no fit state to come in and hurt them. Both girls had some idea of what 'hurt' might mean and were terrified at the thought, but there didn't seem much they could do to stop the men doing whatever they wanted. There were four of them, they were much stronger and it was very obvious they would never listen to pleas for mercy.

'I wonder why they attacked our farm,' Rachel said as she joined her sister at the window.

'I don't know. And why pretend to be Indians? It doesn't make sense.'

'And who was the fifth man? Why did he go back to town?'

Claire shook her head. 'I don't know.'

'Would you know him if you saw him again? I'm not sure I would.'

'I think so.' Claire would certainly recognize the other four.

Three of them were in their early twenties. They had long, untidy hair and greedy eyes. They dressed roughly and smelled of stale whiskey and staler sweat. Nate was the eldest, and he was the leader of the gang. Another two who looked like brothers, were Bobby and Russ, although Claire wasn't sure which was which, although she thought Bobby was the younger of the two.

The fourth man was older, in his late thirties. He was a Mexican, with black greasy hair tucked under a sombrero and a colourful but threadbare serape around his shoulders. He looked the most dangerous of the lot.

'How long are they going to keep us as prisoners?' Rachel clutched at Claire's hand. 'What do they intend to do to us?'

'Someone from Elk Horn will have come to the farm to look for Marshal Detmeyer by now. People will realize we're missing and will come searching for us. They'll find us too, I know they will.'

But would they find them soon enough?

Then they heard the Mexican speak. 'Someone's coming.'

'Oh-oh. It's the boss,' said Nate, 'and he don't look any too pleased.'

'Can you see who it is?' Rachel whispered.

'No.' Claire shook her head. 'But whoever it is they sound awful scared of him!'

13

The sun was already setting by the time Greeley and Walsh reached Elk Canyon, which cut through the hills, twisting and turning between rocks and boulders and the odd clump of trees. Dust rose up from their horses' hooves. Neither man had said much on the ride.

Walsh was aware that Greeley was trying hard to come to terms with the fact that it wasn't Apaches who'd raided the farm and thought it was best to let him get on with it. Meanwhile Greeley was anxious to get back to Elk Horn and find out how Sam Detmeyer was doing.

Before long the scout pulled his horse to a halt and pointed ahead. 'That must be the hovel Archie likes to call a trading post.'

Greeley peered into the gloom and made out an adobe hut, half hidden amongst an outcrop of tall rocks. In front was a corral of sorts. It contained no horses but maybe that was because part of the fence was broken away. That was it. No movement, no sound.

'Don't look like anyone's around,' Walsh went on.

Greeley grunted but didn't reply. He drew his rifle from its scabbard and clicked his horse into a walk. As they got near, he saw that the door of the hut hung half off its hinges and the shutters on the one window were broken.

Walsh grinned. 'Don't take any notice of that. It's the way Archie always lives. Even so he must've moved on. Pity, I'd've liked a couple of words with him.' He slid off his horse and made for the door, Greeley close behind.

At first the gathering darkness made it difficult to see anything inside.

Walsh muttered something to himself and Greeley said, 'He's gone all right. And taken his trade goods with him.'

Except for a blanket on the floor in one corner, and a chair and a pile of dirty clothes and other bits and pieces in the middle of the room, the place was empty.

'Wait up, Gus.'

Greeley felt Walsh grab his arm and pull him forward. And Greeley saw for himself. Something bulky lay under the blanket. Walsh pulled the blanket aside.

'Hell!'

Under it lying on his stomach was the body of a very fat man with greasy shoulder length hair.

'It's Archie!'

'Is he dead?'

Walsh turned the body over.

Archie Ford was dead all right.

His throat had been sliced open and he'd been left to bleed his life out all over the hut's dirt floor.

★   ★   ★

Nate wasn't exactly scared of the man riding into the camp but he was scared

111

enough that he quickly scrambled clumsily to his feet, wishing he hadn't drunk quite as much as he had and his wits weren't quite so befuddled. He kicked the other three up as well. Now he could see that the man was red faced with fury and as he dismounted and strode up to them, his body bristled with anger.

Nate considered himself a bad man, willing to kill for money and pleasure, deserving of the reputation that had resulted in him being wanted dead or alive all over Arizona. As were Russ and Bobby. But this man, The Boss, the one who'd hired them for this job, was something else again.

'You utter bunch of idiots!' said the man by way of greeting. He spoke quietly, which was much worse than if he'd yelled.

None of the others, not even Miguel, whose proud boast it was that he was answerable to no one, said a word. Russ and Bobby made sure to stand well back. Nate was left to act as spokesman.

'Sorry, Boss, what d'you mean?' He was puzzled. 'The raid on the farm went just like you planned. We didn't do nothing to show it wasn't Injuns did it. And we didn't let those cowboys see us so they could be left alive to tell everyone they'd been attacked by Apaches.'

The man smiled. 'Sorry but it didn't go exactly as I said it should. Because in what part of my planning did I tell you fools to take two young girls hostage?'

So that was it!

'I hope it wasn't so you could have your wicked way with them? I really wouldn't like it if it was.'

Nate shook his head. 'We ain't touched 'em.' He didn't admit that that was because they'd all been too drunk. 'We thought it'd make it look even more like an Injun raid cos that's what they did in the old days. Ain't that right, Miguel?'

The Mexican gave a surly nod and an even surlier grin. He couldn't understand this man minding that they might take advantage of two white girls when he wouldn't have minded if they'd been killed. He didn't say so but contented himself with being amused at the way the white boys were shuffling their feet in fear. He was frightened himself but no way was he going to show it.

'Hell! You idiot! That was in the old days. Not now. All you've succeeded in doing is rousing up the townspeople more than they would have been.'

'Ain't that what you wanted?'

'No, not like that!' The man took a step forward forcing Nate, much to his annoyance, to step back. 'It means more people out here searching. They find you they'll know Apaches weren't responsible. You could have spoilt it all.' He glanced at the hut. 'They in there?'

'Yeah.'

'You want us to let 'em go?' Russ asked.

'Let them go? Let them go! You goddamned idiot! When they can identify you and me too maybe? You want to be lynched? Don't be so goddamn stupid. You get rid of them, that's what you do. Like you were meant to get rid of everyone you found at the farm.'

'OK,' Nate said. 'We can do that.'

He hoped that was all but the man's eyes were still glittering and dangerous and now he said, 'And why the hell did you have to shoot the marshal?'

'That wasn't us, that was . . . ' Russ began until his brother, Bobby, poked him in the side.

'He didn't give us no choice,' Nate said. 'He came at us as we were about to ride away.'

'Which he wouldn't have if you'd done the job and ridden away and not stayed to bust things up in the house.'

Nate could have said that wasn't their idea. But he doubted The Boss would want to hear him say out loud who'd been responsible and who'd taken great delight in breaking and smashing whatever he could.

'And, you see, there's another problem. The marshal ain't dead.'

115

'He ain't? But we were sure . . . '

'And he's another one could tell everyone the truth. So deal with him as well.'

'Yessir.'

'And deal with it right, understand? I don't want to hear about any more of your stupid cock-ups! Or else,' the man leant forward pushing his face close to Nate's, 'there'll be hell to pay and I'll have no choice but to deal with you and your mistakes. And you really wouldn't like that. None of you. Have I made myself clear?'

14

'Reckon he's been dead a couple of days at least,' Walsh said after examining the body. 'Varmints have been at him already.'

Greeley could see that for himself. He swallowed hard. He wasn't a squeamish man: that was hardly possible in his line of work, but right now with Archie Ford's bloody corpse lying at his feet he had a sick feeling in the pit of his stomach.

'I'm goin' to take a look outside,' Walsh went on. 'See what I can find.'

'I suppose you want me to bury Ford while you go?'

Walsh shrugged and aimed a light kick at the body.

'Can if you like. Wouldn't bother myself. He ain't an innocent victim like the Bakers. He's done untold damage in his day. To red and white.'

'Even so . . . '

'Once the telegraph is back in action you can let Cap'n Harding know what's happened and he can send men out to deal with Archie. He was always the army's problem rather than anyone else's.'

Greeley saw the sense of that, although he didn't like to think of leaving even someone like Archie Ford, who'd obviously been an unscrupulous crook, unburied. But a glance round revealed nothing that he could use to dig a grave with anyway and he really didn't want to waste any more time or what remained of his energy.

'Wonder who killed him?' Greeley followed Walsh outside, glad to be out in the fresh evening air. He shut the door behind him as best he could.

'Reckon it was whoever traded with him over the bows and arrows.'

'You're sure he was the one who had the weapons to sell?'

Walsh nodded. 'Sure as I can be. Look, Gus, Archie never had much in the way of sense. Seems to me someone came here wanting to buy bows and arrows and Archie realized something bad was about to happen; but also, being extremely greedy, he didn't realize that something bad could also happen to him.'

'He thought to sell the weapons and then get out?'

'Before the army got involved, yeah.'

'But something went wrong.'

'Like I said, Archie was greedy. Mebbe he asked for more'n was offered. Or, more likely, whoever was doing the buying simply didn't want a witness left behind.'

Greeley nodded. 'Makes sense. They've already proved they don't mind killing.'

'Wait there while I take a look round.'

Walsh was soon back.

'Find anything?' asked Greeley.

'Tracks of two horses.'

'Two? Not four or five?'

'No, just the two. Couple of days old.'

'Would that fit in with how long Ford has been dead?'

'Sure would.'

'When they left here, in which direction did they go?'

'Elk Horn.'

* * *

As 'the boss' rode away, the four outlaws breathed sighs of relief, which they tried to hide from one another.

'Hell,' Nate said. He sat down on the ground and took a hefty swig of whiskey before handing the bottle to Russ. 'Don't know what was wrong with him. Thought we did good.' That was the problem with taking orders from other people. They always believed differently and were always complaining. 'Some people ain't never satisfied.'

'Sure ain't,' Miguel, the Mexican, said. 'Don't know why we got involved with him.'

They all knew why. The man had offered to pay them a very generous sum for their help.

'We goin' to do as he says?' Bobby

asked. 'Kill them girls I mean?' He was usually callous enough but to do something like that didn't sit right. Not in cold blood anyway.

'Got a better idea,' Miguel said, with one of his creepy grins. 'Why kill those pretty little ones when we can make good money outta them?'

'How?' Nate asked, interested, as he always was, when money was mentioned.

Another grin. 'I know of a brothel just across the border where good cash, and by that I mean a lot, will always be paid for innocent and young white girls. They're real popular in Mexico. Sass'll soon be whipped out of them there. Soon get 'em straight and earning their keep every night.'

The other three looked at one another and grinned.

'The boss won't like that,' Russ pointed out. 'He wants 'em dead.'

'Hell with that,' Miguel said.

Nate nodded agreement.

'He'll never find out, will he? I don't

see why we shouldn't get paid some more when we're the ones taking all the risks while he sits on his ass and just tells us what to do. C'mon, Russ, Bobby, you must see the sense of it.'

It didn't take much for the two brothers to agree. They'd become outlaws, rather than finding jobs, so as to have plenty of money in their pockets — the more the better — without doing anything like hard work to get it. This scheme would be easy because Miguel would be the one riding to Mexico and back.

'I'll start out first thing in the morning,' Miguel said.

'What about the marshal?' Bobby asked. He didn't mind the thought of killing Detmeyer. He was only a lawman after all, and Bobby didn't like the law.

'I'll do it,' Russ offered.

'You want help?'

'Hell no, Nate, I can manage that on my own. What can a wounded old man do against me? Might even see the doc while I'm in town and get him to fix this 'ere wound.' Damn unlucky shot that was. Bullet grazed his arm. Hurt like hell at first but the whiskey had soon dulled the pain.

'Well, be careful iffen you do.'

'Hell, Nate, I ain't goin' to confess to the doc how come I got shot. I'm sure I can think up some lie to tell him.'

Nate grinned. Despite everything, despite the boss being as scary as hell, everything was working out OK. They could get an even better profit out of this than they'd thought — and kill a lawman to boot.

What could possibly go wrong?

15

'What's up, Gus?' Walsh asked. 'You're awful quiet.'

'Been thinking.'

'Thought so.' Walsh grinned. 'And what have you decided?'

Greeley sighed. 'OK, Henry, I agree with you and Harding that it wasn't Apaches on that raid. It was white men and their motive was probably to get their hands on cheap but good land on the Reservation.'

'Glad you've come round to our way of thinking. But there's something else troubling you, ain't there?'

'Yeah. Why five of 'em? It's unlikely five men would want to start up a ranch together. And why did one of the bastards return to Elk Horn?'

Walsh nodded. 'So?'

'Bastards can always be found willing to shoot and kill innocent people as long as they're paid for it.'

'You believe four of 'em were paid by the one who went back to town?'

'Looks like it to me. Because he is the one wants the land. The one cooked up the scheme. The one in charge.'

Walsh nodded again. 'Yeah, seems likely to me, too. Don't forget, though: two men did for Archie Ford.'

'Perhaps there are two of them in this. Partners in Elk Horn, and only one went out on the Baker farm raid.' Greeley paused to think about that. 'Yes, that could be right.'

'Any idea who?'

'Not yet.'

*　*　*

It was late when Greeley and Walsh finally rode back into Elk Horn.

Gus felt bone-weary and dispirited. He was annoyed because Walsh, despite being so much older than him, seemed to be bearing up better.

They left their equally tired horses at

the livery stable and walked through the town to the marshal's office. Greeley was a bit surprised that Walsh stayed with him and didn't go on about his own business. He decided it was probably so that he could keep an eye on the situation and try to make sure no one blamed the Apaches for something they hadn't done.

Eddie Smith was sitting alone at his desk. Greeley asked him how Sam Detmeyer was.

'No change last time I heard. By the way, when Old Man Simpson went out to the Baker farm to see to the animals he found the marshal's horse wandering about nearby. He caught it up and brought it back to town.'

Greeley frowned. 'I suppose Sam didn't tether it properly in all the commotion and it ran off.'

'Ann . . . '

'Eddie, I really don't think Marshal Detmeyer would be pleased to hear you calling his daughter by just her Christian name,' Greeley interrupted with a grin. Eddie went bright red and gulped several times.

'Er, Miss Detmeyer. Miss Detmeyer is very worried. Not only about her father but also about Claire and Rachel.'

'OK, I'll go and see her as soon as I can.'

'Did you have any luck finding the girls or the bastards that killed their family?'

'No, not really.' Quickly Greeley told him all that he and Walsh had done that day. He didn't think they'd achieved much despite the long hours spent in the saddle. Eddie glanced from one to the other of them.

'A telegram came in from Captain Harding about thirty minutes ago.'

'Good. That means his men have mended the line.'

'It was only down in one place.'

Greeley was aware of Walsh looking at him as if to say that didn't sound like Indians. Eddie picked up a piece of paper from his desk.

'His troops found no sign of the Baker girls or any trail of the raiders.'

'I expect they're still over in the direction of Five-Mile Valley,' Walsh put in.

'Yeah, the captain thinks the same but they'll go out tomorrow to look round some more near the fort just in case. And,' he glanced down at the message, 'Harding has spoken to Talking Bear, one of the tribal leaders. He confirms that no Apaches have left the Reservation in the last few days. Harding says Talking Bear is honest and he believes him.'

'I doubt Talking Bear would lie over something serious like this,' Walsh put in. 'I knew him in the old days,' he added with a smile. 'Real old rabble rouser he was back then, always the first one to put on war paint. Chased him all the way into Mexico once with him causing havoc every step of the way.'

Greeley frowned. He didn't think that warranted the affection Walsh obviously felt for the Indian.

'When he saw that the Apaches couldn't possibly win against the white hordes, he changed to a path of peace. Gus, he's followed it ever since. He only wants what's best for his people.'

'Despite what Harding said, I sent out messages to the towns round about warning them to be on their guard like you wanted, Mr Greeley. So far nothing has come back from anyone to say they've suffered an attack.'

'That's because there ain't any Indian attacks.'

'It ain't what people in town are saying,' Eddie said. Despite what Greeley had told him, he sounded as if it wasn't really what he was saying either.

'Then we've gotta put 'em right. Look, son, this is real serious. None of us want any Indian trouble stirred up again, not after it's been so quiet for such a long while. Not when they ain't done nothing.'

'Are those two cowboys who were attacked still here?' Greeley asked. 'I'd like to talk to them if so.'

Eddie nodded. 'They sure are. They're with the rest of the white hordes causing their own havoc in The Antlers.'

16

'Damn Apaches!'

'Damn Injuns! They want stringing up.'

'What's the damn army doing about 'em?'

'Taking good land and killing innocent white farmers.'

'And kidnapping women and children. Violating their purity.'

When Greeley, followed by a worried-looking Eddie Smith and an even more worried Walsh, pushed his way into The Antlers, it was to find the saloon full of red-faced, angry men. They were pushing and shoving and shouting at one another in loud voices.

'Hell!' Walsh muttered. 'It's just like it was after the War. They'll be calling for the extermination of the whole tribe soon. Or offering bounties on Apache scalps. It just ain't right.'

Jack Phillips yelled for quiet and banged on the bar until he got it. The crowd in front of him shifted a little and Greeley could see that Josephine was standing by her brother's side, a smug look on her face; in front of him were two men he hadn't seen before but who, along with Jack and Josephine, were the obvious ringleaders, the ones who were calling for action.

'David and Will Preston,' Eddie said in his ear. 'And see behind them — they're the two cowboys who were attacked.'

The two young men were clearly enjoying their moment of fame.

'What are we going to do about this outrage? We must do something,' Preston began, his clear voice echoing round the room and bringing nods of agreement and some arm-waving. 'We cannot let the Apaches kill and rob and raid and then return to their Reservation knowing they will be safe from retribution. If we don't do something now it will keep on happening and more innocent people will suffer.'

Yells of agreement.

'Moreover, they're squatting on land suitable for farming. When they have no idea of what farming means and all they want to do is hunt.'

More yells.

'Fat chance when most of the game has been driven away,' Walsh said.

'There are a lot of us could use that land,' Will Preston said.

He was about twenty-five, five years younger than David and enough like him for Greeley to have known they were brothers without being told. He was a bit shorter than David, rail-thin, and he had a moustache and bushy hair. He was also dressed casually in jeans and plaid shirt.

'We sure could,' Phillips added. 'Land on which to grow crops is in short supply these days.'

'As is land for prize cattle,' Preston said. 'Those damn Apaches are sitting on all that prime land down by the river and not using it.'

'That ain't true.' Walsh shouldered his way to the front of the crowd, Greeley and Eddie close behind.

'Oh-oh,' Phillips sneered. 'Here comes the goddamned Injun-lover. Well, suppose we'd better hear what the squaw-man has to say.'

This was followed by jeers and cat-calls.

'Listen to me. The tribe on the Reservation are farming their land as best they can with what the government has given 'em.'

Preston took no notice but shouted above the noise:

'Ah, but we all know that what they like to do best is ride out whenever they want to, because the army doesn't even try to stop them, to butcher decent white folks. Men, women and children.'

Many more yells and stamping of feet.

'Even worse, two young girls have been kidnapped. God only knows what is happening to them right now. It makes my blood freeze to think of them in the hands of those red devils.'

'That's not true either,' Greeley said. 'We have it on the authority of Captain Harding' — a few more catcalls — 'that no Apache has left the Reservation for days. They're not responsible for the killings or the kidnapping.'

'Then tell us,' Preston said, almost poking Greeley in the chest but thinking better of it when he saw the glint in the other man's eyes, 'who the hell was responsible for the raid out at the Baker farm?'

'Yeah! Yeah!'

'I don't know yet but it wasn't Apaches.'

'Yeah, it must've been.' One of the cowboys, Pete, pushed his way to the bar. 'They attacked us. We heard their yips and Mike here,' he clapped his friend on the shoulder, 'was shot in the leg with an arrow. Just like the Baker family.'

'That's right.' Preston nodded. 'Are you calling them liars? Why would they lie? Ask the doctor. He fixed young

Mike here up. He can tell you.'

'It was real frightening,' Mike added. 'We thought we were dead for sure. There must have been at least twenty of the bastards trying to kill us.'

'It's a wonder, if there were so many of them, that they didn't finish the job then,' Greeley said sarcastically. 'Or were you so brave and such good shots you scared 'em off?'

There were a few laughs at this.

Both young men reddened with anger and embarrassment; they knew they hadn't been brave at all.

'Did you actually see any Apaches?' Walsh asked.

'Yes,' said Mike.

'No,' said Pete.

'Make up your minds.'

'No,' Pete admitted. 'No, we didn't. We heard 'em and, like I said, we were shot at. That's all true. But it was too dark to actually see who was doing it.'

Mike added, 'But why would anyone pretend to be an Indian shooting at us? Don't make sense.'

'That's right, it doesn't,' Will Preston said, frowning, not having liked the way the conversation had gone. 'Of course it must have been Apaches who attacked them. They're probably getting ready to attack other farms right now. Maybe even Elk Horn itself.'

Walsh sneered. 'Don't be stupid.'

Will took a step closer to the old scout before his brother stopped him.

'If the army won't help us then we should do something for ourselves,' Phillips spoke up. 'Make sure the powers that be know we mean business.'

'Be careful, all of you,' Greeley said. His gaze encompassed those in the saloon. 'If you listen to these men and take the law into your own hands, you'll be the ones in trouble.'

Phillips interrupted. 'What would you know about the law? You ain't nothing but a damn bounty hunter.'

'That's as maybe, but I don't break the law.'

Preston swung round on Eddie. 'Well

then, Deputy, what the hell is the law doing about this outrage?'

'It's in hand,' Greeley said. 'The army has been informed. They're ready to act if need be. Against whoever is responsible. And against whoever decides to go up against the Indians at the Reservation.'

'Well, that's just fine. I'd like to know what they are going to do to help us.'

'That's right,' Phillips said with a little nod. 'The law and the army don't care about the likes of us.'

But glancing round, Greeley could see that most of the crowd were losing interest in the argument. None of them would have any objection to taking their chances by going up against the Indians, but where the army was concerned it was a different matter. The army was well organized and well armed. A mob would be no match for a group of cavalrymen.

Phillips, who knew his customers, realized the same. He contented himself with scowling at Greeley and Walsh.

'Just watch yourselves. Folks round

here don't like those who take the side of damn Injuns against decent white folks.' He pointed a finger at Walsh. 'And, you, don't come back into my saloon. You and your kind ain't welcome.'

'Suits me. Don't come in here much anyway. I don't like the company either.'

Greeley glanced at Josephine. She didn't say anything. Presumably he and his money were still welcome in the brothel.

'That was a close-run thing,' Eddie said when they went outside into the cool air of the night.

'I shouldn't worry,' Greeley told him. 'That crowd in there can't cause any real trouble. If they'd gotten anywhere near the Reservation, the army would've ridden out and dealt with them.'

'They might do some damage if they're egged on by someone who stays in the background and doesn't much care if they get hurt or not,' Walsh pointed out. 'You and me had better ride out again in the morning. Try to find that trail we lost.'

'OK,' Greeley agreed.

17

David Preston watched Greeley and his two cohorts leave the saloon. Everything had been going so well, but now, like Phillips, he knew it would be useless to try to whip the crowd up into a fury. They'd gone back to drinking, talking to the girls and listening to the piano player, while several were already leaving.

'Who was that?' he asked Phillips. 'The younger one.'

'Gustavus Greeley. He's a bounty hunter. Pretty good at his job, too. More often than not he catches whoever he goes after and more often than not he brings 'em in slung over the back of a horse. He's sort of pals with the marshal, too.'

'And the other one? The one you said was an Indian-lover.'

'He sure sounded like one to me,'

Will put in with one of his scowls.

'Henry Walsh. Used to be an army scout. I shouldn't worry about either one of 'em. Walsh is pretty harmless these days. He might still be able to follow a trail but that's about all. He ain't been involved in a fight for years. As for Greeley, he's only interested in doing something if money is involved.'

'That right?' It hadn't looked that way to Preston. Maybe Phillips believed it because money was what made his world go round and he thought everyone was the same.

'Sure is.'

'David, I'm bored,' Will whined. 'Keene is starting up a poker game.' He indicated the table where the gambler employed at The Antlers was shuffling cards. 'I'm going to play a game or two.'

'OK Don't lose all your money.'

'I won't. Tonight is my lucky night.'

Preston decided he'd better stay.

★ ★ ★

Roger Keene could hardly be taken for anything but a gambler. He had long and curly fair hair and wide moustaches and wore a variety of brightly coloured vests. He'd been in town since the spring and, being a good poker player, had made a great deal of money for himself and for the Phillips brother and sister: Jack always took a cut from any winnings while Josephine charged him for a room to sleep in at the brothel.

He was an honest player, although Phillips was always going on at him to cheat if necessary rather than lose, which was a blow to his considerable pride, as he was also a clever player. Luckily mostly the gamblers he'd come across in Elk Horn were so easy to beat he didn't need to resort to tricks to win. They also took their losses with a good grace and in the forlorn hope that next time they might stand a chance of winning.

All, that was, except for the new-comer to town: Will Preston.

He'd played five-card stud with

Keene a couple of times before. As he was nowhere near as good a player as he thought himself, never knowing when it was best to fold or raise, never keeping an eye on what cards had been played, he nearly always lost. Quite heavily, too. He didn't like that. Not one bit. He had a wildness in his eyes and a temper to match. So far he hadn't caused a ruckus but there was always a first time.

So now when Keene saw the young man headed his way his heart sank and he made sure he could get at the derringer he kept in his vest pocket quickly and easily. Feelings had been running high all night because of the attack on the Baker farm and tonight was when matters could spill over into trouble.

Will sat down.

'Play,' he ordered and placed several coins on the table in front of him.

Keene would have liked to tell him to get lost — he didn't like being spoken to rudely — but Phillips wouldn't like that. A glance at the bar showed the pro that the man was watching him, ready to complain. So he dealt out the cards and, together with the other two men at the table, they started the game.

'Cards, gentlemen?'

'Three,' Will said, scowling at his hand.

That was another thing. He didn't possess a good poker face. Keene could always tell whether he had a decent hand or not.

Tonight, as Keene feared, Will was more reckless than ever. He bet heavily and lost heavily too; not winning even one game. Most of his money went to Keene, who was secretly pleased to be besting the impatient and impulsive young man, but he lost to the others as well.

About an hour later Will threw down his hand.

'Goddammit! You win again!' He leaned forward and eyed Keene. 'You sure you ain't cheating me?'

A hush fell upon the crowd and the

two men at the table quickly backed away.

'No, I'm not,' Keene said as smoothly as he could, all the while his hand inching towards the derringer.

'Well, I think you are. Your luck ain't natural. No one can be that lucky.'

'Son, don't start trouble you might have difficulty finishing.'

'Hell . . . '

Things could have turned nasty quickly. Keene's gun was halfway out of his vest pocket. Will's hand was reaching towards his own gun. Keene would beat him to the draw and he wouldn't hesitate to shoot. Not only did he have his reputation to protect but he was aware that the other man was quite willing to fire his gun.

'No, he's not cheating.' David Preston was suddenly there by the table. He pushed his brother back down. 'Will, Mr Keene here is winning fair and square. I've been watching him most of the evening and it's simply that he's a good player. A much better one than you. Also better than these other gentlemen, isn't that right?'

The two gamblers gave nervous laughs and nodded.

'Now, drink up your beer and we'll get going. It's late. Goodnight, Mr Keene, I'm sorry about this. My brother can be a bit hot-headed at times but he doesn't mean any real harm.'

Keene nodded, accepting the apology because he had no choice. He didn't miss the hate-filled glare that Will sent his way. Will wasn't going to forget this in a hurry. Suddenly tired, he threw down his cards.

'Game's over, gentlemen. I'm retiring for the night. I suggest you do the same.'

He headed for the brothel next door.

* * *

Russ decided to wait just outside Elk Horn until he was sure that the place had closed up for that Sunday evening. He would have liked to visit the

146

red-light district and have a beer and a woman but he decided that neither Nate nor the boss would approve and he didn't quite dare.

He knew where Marshal Detmeyer lived. The boss had told them that. When the time came he'd leave his horse in the main street by the real-estate office rather than by the marshal's house. That way it wouldn't be too far for him to make a quick escape, neither would it be spotted by a nosy neighbour.

Not that he expected any trouble. No one would anticipate an attack on the marshal in his own home when he was lying in bed recovering from being wounded by an Apache. Russ stifled a giggle at that.

No, he'd break in, kill the lawman and be out again before anyone was any the wiser.

Easy!

18

'Melissa, do you know anything about the Preston brothers?' Greeley asked.

The two of them were sitting in the brothel's parlour, enjoying some of Josephine's best whiskey. Greeley had money enough to pay for both drink and girl but tonight he didn't have the energy to go to bed with Melissa. Anyway sometimes it was nice just to sit with her and talk. She was pleasant company. Besides, he had to be away soon to go and see how Sam was doing. Really he should have gone before this but he'd given in to his want for a drink and his desire to see Melissa.

The girl thought for a moment or two.

'The older one, David, has never been here as a client. Will has, but he's never asked for anyone in particular. He's just gone with whoever was available, and that's never been me. From what I've heard they've come here from Kansas and are looking to buy land to start up a ranch, as they think that's where the money is. They're angry because they're having difficulty in finding suitable land to buy.'

'How long have they been in town?'

'Umm, about three months. Yeah, that's right. They arrived in early April. They rent a property over near the marshal's. As far as I know they've never caused any trouble, although Will has come close a time or two and . . . ' She paused in raising her glass.

'What is it?'

'Evidently their eldest brother was killed at the Battle of Chickamauga and Will's greatest regret is that he was too young to fight in the Civil War. Or to come West when the Indians were stirring up trouble, and fight them.' She laughed. 'He thinks he's tough and reckless and can see himself as a colonel in the cavalry shouting *Charge!* Josephine had to throw him out last time he was here as he was so drunk he'd started to annoy and frighten Kate. Josephine threatened him with calling in the marshal. I doubt she would have done but, not for the first time, David came to the rescue and took him home.'

Will Preston was obviously a trouble-maker and had only escaped getting involved with the law by the skin of his teeth and his brother's help.

The door opened and Roger Keene came in.

'You're early tonight,' Melissa said.

'Get me a drink, hon, I need it. Hi there, Gus.' Keene took the glass of whiskey Melissa poured for him while she also took the chance to fill up Greeley's glass as well as her own. 'Nearly had a run in with Will Preston! He accused me of cheating.'

'We were just talking about him, weren't we, Gus?'

'Luckily his brother saved the day, again, or I might've had to shoot the silly bastard. He's a useless poker player but he wants to blame everyone else for his mistakes. 'Course Jack just stood behind the bar and watched. Didn't do nothing as usual.'

'I wonder you're still working at The Antlers,' Greeley said as the man sat opposite them. 'The way you feel about Jack I'd've thought you'd've left by now.'

'I'm not staying much longer. Just another month or so while there're still plenty of players willing to lose to me, then I'm off and heading someplace where I don't have to work for Mr Skinflint. I'm the one with the gambling skills. He's the one insists on taking a cut. Old bastard. Probably I'll head for Tucson. I hear tell that's a nice place. Be hot in the winter, too.'

Melissa said, 'A girl from here, a friend, saved enough money to buy a boarding house there. She's doing well. She's respectable now and even gets to go to church on a Sunday.' She sounded wistful. Keene smiled at her.

'Hey, Gus, heard you were involved

151

in that bad business over at the Baker farm. How's Sam?'

'From what Doc says he'll pull through.'

'That's good. Can't say me and the law always see eye to eye but Sam is fairer than most. What about the two girls?'

'Me and Henry Walsh are riding out again tomorrow to try and find some trace of them.'

'I hope you do,' Melissa said. 'It's terrible to think of them out there, all alone and prisoners of the men who killed their family, and how scared they must be. More whiskey, Roger?'

Because Keene had so little time for Phillips, Greeley knew he'd be quite willing to talk to him, answer his questions. So now he said,

'Were you in The Antlers on Saturday afternoon?'

'Sure. I don't usually bother to play afternoons but Saturdays are different. Ranch owners and cowboys start drifting in around noon and they're always eager for a game of cards and the chance to lose their money. Which they always do.'

Greeley grinned at the man's boasting.

'Jack there?'

'Yeah.'

'All the time?'

'Don't know. Sorry, what I meant was, Jack was in his office at the back going over reports and orders.'

'Funny time to be doing that when the saloon was likely to be busy.'

'No better time for it according to Jack.' Keene drank some of his whiskey. 'He don't like hard work. He sees several customers coming through the door he skedaddles quick and leaves someone else to serve them.'

'Josephine often says the same,' Melissa added.

'Did anyone see him there? Go in to speak to him?'

Keene leant forward. 'Believe me, Gus, when he's in his office no one, besides his silly sister, and I mean no

153

one, dares go in to disturb him. Last 'tender who did that was fired on the spot. He'd only gone in to warn Jack that trouble was brewing with a couple of merry cowboys. Guess Jack'd only want to be interrupted iffen the place was on fire and he was in danger of being caught in the flames.'

'So you don't know for sure if he was in there or not?'

'Saw him go through the door, saw him come out again.' Keene shrugged. 'But as there's a second door in the office that leads to the saloon's back door so he can make a quick escape if needs be, then, no, I ain't got a notion of what the hell he was up to all afternoon.' His eyes narrowed. 'Why all the questions?'

'Henry Walsh and Captain Harding at the fort believe that someone is trying to drive the Apaches off their Reservation to free up their land.'

'But that's awful,' Melissa cried. 'You mean the Baker family were killed over land?'

'And you think old Jack might be involved in some way?' asked Keene.

Greeley shrugged. 'The Phillipses are after selling their businesses to start up a ranch. They were certainly stirring up the crowd in the saloon tonight.'

'When Josephine came back she said it had all got a bit heated and she seemed quite pleased it had,' Melissa said. 'She was in a real good mood for once.'

'Yeah, but them two on a ranch!' Keene said. 'Pie in the sky iffen you ask me anything.'

Melissa said, 'But just because they'd surely fail at ranching doesn't mean they wouldn't be stupid enough to try.'

'Jack's his own boss too, and can come and go whenever he likes without anyone being any the wiser.'

'True enough.' Keene sat back in his chair and frowned. 'Much as I'd like to believe it of him, because nothing would give me greater pleasure than seeing the bastard in jail and on the way to the hangman, I can't see it, Gus. Not really. I can't see Jack whooping it up like an Apache and firing arrows at people. He's a coward at heart.'

'I agree, but he could have gone along on the raid to tell the others what to do. There was a fifth man with the gang, who rode back alone to Elk Horn.'

'Dunno how you'd prove any of it.'

Nor did Greeley.

'He your only suspect?'

'No. There are the Preston brothers.'

'Yeah, likely. They too were shouting the odds in the saloon.'

'Were the Preston brothers in there on Saturday?'

'Not in the afternoon, no. As for the evening I can't say I noticed them. But, Gus, it was real busy and I was playing poker with some serious players for once. That took all my attention.'

'They all bear keeping an eye on,' Greeley said. Also, of course, there might well be others in town or round about who had the same idea and the same motive.

'I just hope there's no more trouble,' Melissa said.

Greeley hoped so too, but he wouldn't bet on it.

'Drink up, sweetheart, I'd better let you get back to the paying customers, keep Josephine sweet tempered. And I've got to go and see how Sam is doing.'

'Good luck,' Keene called as Greeley kissed Melissa goodnight and let himself out of the brothel.

19

Russ stopped at the corner of the quiet street that was lined with the houses of Elk Horn's wealthier citizens. And changed his mind about what he was going to do.

Now he was actually here and able to see the layout of the street, he decided, for once, to act sensibly. Although he liked the thought of it, it wouldn't be a good idea to crash in through the front door and start shooting. Before he could get away, nosy neighbours could put in an appearance. Even walking down the road, someone across the way could be looking out of a window and spot him, a stranger, and wonder what he was up to. He might be challenged and stopped before he could kill the marshal. No way did he want Nate, and especially not The Boss, accusing him of botching what should be a simple job.

No, best to get into the house from the back where he wouldn't be seen.

And it would be better to use a knife to kill Detmeyer. That would be silent as well as quick.

He soon found a narrow pathway that ran along the backs of the houses, divided from them by low adobe walls and small, well-kept gardens. The riverbank was on the other side. Whatever noise he made wouldn't be heard above the rush of the river. Nor was anyone about.

He smiled: this was a good plan. He was so good at planning he often thought he should be the leader of the gang rather than Nate, who just liked to ride in shooting and hope for the best. Perhaps with Bobby's help he'd make a play for the position and soon, although he wasn't sure what Miguel would have to say about it. Miguel didn't like him but then he didn't much like anyone. With luck the Mexican would stay in Mexico with the little white girls and, although that meant they could say goodbye to any more money, good riddance to him.

There — that was Detmeyer's house!

It was in darkness except for the glow of a candle in one window; probably the room where the marshal was lying injured. It was no use getting in at the bedroom window, Detmeyer might have recovered enough to be awake, in which case he could raise the alarm. No, best to break in at the unlit window.

Earlier in the evening Ann had told Mrs Hooper she didn't need anyone to sit with her any longer.

Her father was improving all the time, had in fact opened his eyes at one point, demanded a drink of water and promptly gone back to sleep. He was going to be all right. And she knew that Mrs Hooper had remained awake all last night.

'You need your rest, too,' Ann had told her.

Now it was getting late. Ann was tired and she stood up from her seat by her father's bed and kissed his cheek.

'Goodnight, Papa,' she whispered. 'I'm going to bed now. I'll see you in the morning.'

And that was when she heard the sound of rattling at the parlour window. Someone was trying to get in.

For a moment she was sure she must be imagining things. This couldn't be happening. But no — there was the sound again. It was followed by something breaking and a muttered curse. Her heart hammered with fear. Who was it? What did they want? Whoever it was they were up to no good. Meant her and her father harm. And she was alone. Why oh why had she sent Mrs Hooper away?

With hands that shook so badly they seemed to have a life of their own, she reached into the drawer of the chest by her father's bed. It was where he kept his pistol within easy reach, ready and loaded. With difficulty she freed it from the holster. He'd taught her to shoot when she was a little girl and made her practice at least once a week. She was now a reasonably good shot, although, of course, she'd never fired a gun in anger or fear. Never shot at anyone before.

Could she do so now?

Trembling, she let herself out of the room and came face to face with a young man standing in the hallway, knife in his hand and gleeful excitement on his face. His look changed to one of utter surprise as he saw her but then he laughed.

'Two for the price of one,' he said and raised his knife.

Ann screamed once very loud and fired the gun.

Halfway down the street, Greeley came to a startled halt.

'What the hell?' he muttered.

At the same time he realized it must be Ann Detmeyer who had screamed. It had been followed by a shot. She and Sam were in danger. He didn't hesitate. Cursing himself for having delayed so long in coming here, he drew his gun and took off at a run. Leapt the picket fence and raced up to the porch. There had been no more cries but as he got to the door he could hear the sounds of a scuffle. He kicked open the door and plunged inside.

Two people were struggling in the hallway. Ann and a young man. Greeley didn't dare shoot for fear of hitting Ann. 'Hey! Stop that!' he yelled. 'Stop right there!'

The young man looked up, swore nastily and hit Ann round the jaw. She fell to the floor with a cry of pain and shock.

And her attacker pushed by Greeley and raced out of the front door.

'You OK?' Greeley paused by Ann. 'He didn't hurt you, did he?'

She shook her head, momentarily unable to speak.

'Or Sam?'

'No. Get him,' she gasped.

Greeley touched her shoulder and started after the intruder.

Russ couldn't believe this. First the

girl had shot at him, the bullet sizzling past his ear, almost hitting him. And when he'd grabbed her and tried to get the gun from her she'd put up a fight, kicking and biting. Then someone had arrived to help her.

It wasn't fair.

He'd failed to kill the marshal — he'd never take over from Nate now, might be in danger from The Boss, who'd made it plain he didn't like to be thwarted. And he certainly was in danger of being caught and killed. Caught, he'd face the hangman. He made up his mind.

Might as well make a fight of it. He was, after all, a pretty good shot.

20

Greeley put all his efforts into giving chase. He had no intention of letting the intruder, whoever he was, escape.

He wanted to catch him and when he did he would find out who he was, what he was up to and whether it had anything to do with the attack on the Baker farm. Best to stop the man before he reached Main Street because once there he might find a place to hide. Greeley would catch him eventually; it would just take more time.

Oh-oh!

All at once the man stopped, turned round and fired his gun.

Greeley skidded to a halt and flung himself to the ground. He rolled to one side as two more shots followed.

His quarry was a good shot. He might not miss again. Especially once he'd steadied himself.

Greeley had wanted to bring th young man in alive to question him but he was left with no choice.

From a prone position, he lifted his own gun, took careful aim and fired: once, twice. The other man doubled up, let out a cry of shock and pain, and crumpled to the ground. He didn't move.

Oh lord, Detmeyer was not going to like this! A shootout in Elk Horn and a dead body in the street where he lived.

Greeley got up and approached the body carefully. Several people were coming out of the nearby houses, demanding to know what was going on. Among them was Doctor Hooper. Gus signalled to everyone to move back, in case the young man was faking his death and getting ready to shoot again. But close up it was clear that he wasn't. Both bullets had taken him in the chest, close to the heart. Greeley beckoned the doctor forward.

'It's OK, folks,' Hooper said. 'No need for alarm. I know Mr Greeley nere.' He touched Gus on the shoulder.

'What's the shooting about?' some-one called out.

'I'm not exactly sure. Except this man,' Greeley poked the body with his foot, 'was in Sam's house, threatening Ann. He had a knife.'

'What!' Hooper cried. 'Is she hurt?'

'He hit her in the face.' Another harder poke.

'What about the marshal?'

'She said he was OK When I got there she was struggling with this 'un. Even fired a gun at him.'

'God. Hey you.' Hooper signalled to one of his neighbours. 'Get my wife to go into Sam Detmeyer's. Ann shouldn't be left alone. And someone else fetch the deputy.'

Two men ran off to do his bidding.

Hooper crouched down by the body, examining it.

'You ever seen him before? Know who he is?'

'No.' Hooper shook his head. 'I don't remember seeing him around town.

Not the respectable part anyhow. Wait up!'

'What is it?'

'Look, there's blood on his sleeve.'

Greeley was puzzled. 'I only fired twice.' Then he added, 'Perhaps Ann's shot grazed him.'

Hooper ripped the sleeve of the man's shirt.

'No, see, this is from an earlier wound. It's been patched up roughly, and obviously, what with struggling with Ann and then running from you, the wound opened up and started to bleed again. Gus, didn't you say that one of the attackers out at the Baker place was shot?'

'Yeah. So this man is one of the so-called Apaches. Damn! Wish I'd just winged the bastard. We could've learnt a lot from him.'

Hooper stood up and reached out a hand towards Greeley.

'Don't blame yourself for that. It's dark and he was shooting at you. You couldn't take the time or the chance to

168

:y to wound him.'

Greeley didn't think he was that good a shot anyway, although he didn't admit it.

'Don't rush to conclusions. It's likely sure that he's one of the raiders but at the same time the marshal has made a number of enemies in his job. This could be someone he arrested in the past, out for revenge.'

'It's a bit of a coincidence though,' Greeley said. 'I don't like coincidences.'

But why risk coming here to attack Sam?

'If they thought Sam could recognize them, the bastards wouldn't want him alive as a witness.'

'Perhaps you're right,' Hooper agreed with a nod. 'Look, can I leave you to wait for the deputy and the undertaker while I go and make sure that both Ann and her father are safe and unhurt?'

'OK. Oh, here comes Eddie now.'

The deputy arrived at a run.

'What the hell is going on?' he demanded; then as he saw the dead

169

body, added, 'Mr Greeley! I might've known you'd be at the heart of any trouble. Is Ann ... er ... Miss Detmeyer, that is ... is she all right?'

★   ★   ★

It was almost an hour later before Greeley got back to the marshal's house. As well as waiting for the undertaker, he'd had to help Eddie disperse the crowd and reassure others who'd come to see what was happening that everything was all right and back to normal and they should go on home. He was relieved to learn that Detmeyer hadn't been hurt, thanks to his daughter, and that Ann was all right too, except for bruises on her arm and a large purple bruise and even larger lump disfiguring her face. She was also very scared.

'She's in bed,' Hooper said. 'But she wouldn't take anything to help her sleep as she was determined to stay awake until you got here.'

'I'll stay for the rest of the night,' Greeley said. 'No need for either you or Mrs Hooper to do so. I'll keep them both safe.'

'We'll say goodnight then.'

Once they'd gone Greeley went into the girl's bedroom — and God only knew what Detmeyer would have to say about that!

'How are you?' He smiled.

'Better now you're here.'

'Good. You were very brave. You saved your father's life. Now best try to get some sleep. And don't worry. I'm not going anywhere. Not tonight. I'll be asleep in the hall. You'll be perfectly safe. Come morning Eddie is going to get someone to fix your window and the door.'

'Thank you, Mr Greeley.'

'My pleasure.'

21

It was still dark when Greeley woke up. Suddenly. A noise from Detmeyer's bedroom had disturbed him.

Immediately alert, he got up from his uncomfortable position lying on the hard floor, and looked in at the door. By the light of the candle he saw that Detmeyer was awake and trying to sit up.

'Don't.' He went to the bed and pushed the man back down.

'What are you doing here, Gus? At night.'

Greeley smiled at hearing the marshal's suspicious tone of voice.

'There's gratitude for you. I'm protecting your ass. No! I said don't get up. You've been badly hurt.'

'I can see that.' Detmeyer looked down at the bandages criss-crossing his chest.

'How d'you feel?'

'Thirsty as hell.'

'Here.' Greeley poured out a glass of water and held it to Detmeyer's lips. 'Careful. Not too much.'

Detmeyer collapsed back on to the pillows.

'What the hell happened to me? Everything hurts and I feel so weak. Where's Ann? Is she all right?'

'Yeah, she is.' Greeley paused, then went on rather awkwardly, 'But, well, look, first of all you should know that someone broke in last night. They were obviously trying to kill you and Ann was here alone. She was hurt . . . '

'What!'

'It's OK. Not badly. I got here in time to prevent that. And you don't have to worry. I dealt with the bastard.'

'Shot him you mean?'

'Yeah. I didn't have a choice.'

Greeley's grimace wasn't needed.

'Good,' Detmeyer said. For once he didn't criticize the bounty hunter. Anyone who threatened his daughter deserved to die.

'Wait up. I'll get her.' Greeley went into the hallway and called, 'Ann. Ann, your pa is awake.'

The girl appeared almost at once, shrugging into a dressing-gown. Detmeyer swore under his breath when he saw her bruised and swollen face and blackened eye.

'Papa!' She flung herself down by the bed and began to cry. 'Oh, Papa, I thought I'd lose you.'

Detmeyer stroked her hair. 'No chance of that, sweetheart. I'm too ornery to die. I'm all right. But if someone don't tell me what's going on right now this very minute I will most certainly not be all right. I shall be so damn angry I won't be responsible for what I do or say!'

'Papa, language.' Ann kissed his forehead. 'Mr Greeley will explain everything while I get you some of the beef tea Doctor Hooper prescribed to build up your strength.'

'Beef tea!' Detmeyer exclaimed in

disgust. 'I can't drink that muck! That's for old men and invalids.'

'Which you are at the moment,' Greeley said, laughing. 'Do you good.'

'You'll drink it and that's an end of it,' added Ann.

'And I'll tell your stubborn father why he can't get out of bed just yet or go to The Antlers for a shot of rotgut whiskey.'

'While you're at it you put some clothes on, missy,' Detmeyer called after his daughter. 'You're undressed in front of Mr Greeley.'

'Oh, Pa! You're clearly getting back to normal already.'

'OK, Gus, you just tell me what's been happening.'

So while Ann was making the dreaded beef tea, Greeley quickly told Detmeyer about the attack on the Baker farm and how he'd found the marshal shot and wounded in the farmyard.

'With an arrow in my back?' Detmeyer was incredulous.

'Yeah. What do you remember?'

Detmeyer thought for a while. 'I remember riding up to the farm. Barn was still burning and I knew right off something was real wrong. Then, yeah, then I heard cries and screams coming from the yard at the back. I'd already dismounted to go into the house but instead I ran round to find out what was going on.' He broke off with a frown. 'That's about it. Was that when I was shot?'

'It's where I found you.' Greeley let the marshal have some more water. 'Did you see the men responsible? Could you identify them?'

'I only got a glimpse of 'em. They were strangers to me, Gus, but what I do know is that they sure as hell weren't Indians. There were three young white men and an older Mexican. So why the hell were they using bows and arrows?'

'To make it look like an Apache raid and stir up trouble.'

Detmeyer swore, then asked, 'Has it?'

'Sort of. But we've got it under control. For now anyway.'

'I sure as hell hope so. Who's *we*?'

'Me and Eddie. And Henry Walsh.'

'Oh yeah. He's a good man.' Detmeyer closed his eyes and Greeley thought he was going back to sleep. Then he opened them again and said, 'D'you have any idea of who the bastards were?'

'No. But, you see, it seems whoever is responsible doesn't just want to stir up trouble. They want to get the Reservation taken away from the Indians. Good land there.'

Detmeyer nodded his understanding. 'Who?'

'I don't know. But I've got some ideas.'

'Who?' Detmeyer repeated.

'Sure you're up to all this?'

'Get on with it,' Detmeyer growled.

'There's two newcomers to town. David and Will Preston. Know them?'

'Sort of. David Preston introduced himself to me as soon as they got here. Said he and his brother were keen to start up a ranch. They haven't caused any trouble since. In fact I heard tell that David was after joining the town council.'

'Real civic-minded.'

'Some people are, Gus. Why do you suspect them?'

'Just a gut feeling, really.' Greeley had learned not to dismiss his instincts; listening to them had saved his life on more than one occasion. 'They were stirring it up in The Antlers the other night. Along with Jack and Josephine Phillips, who could also be guilty.'

'Why on earth would you think those two might be responsible?'

'They want to quit the business they're in and start farming.' To Gus's surprise Detmeyer laughed — or tried to until a wince of pain stopped him. 'What's so funny?'

'Oh, Gus, they've been talking about selling up and going into farming for years. It's never happened and it never will. Can you imagine Jack getting up at five in the morning every day of the year to care for his livestock? Or

Josephine up to her neck in mud while she looks after the pigs?'

Greeley laughed in his turn. 'Put like that, no, I can't.'

'Besides they're real suited to what they do. It's just that they like to moan and complain all the time about how hard the work is. Be a damn sight harder on a farm. They're both full of bluster.'

'Even so, I have found out that Jack could've left the saloon on Saturday afternoon, with no one any the wiser when the raid was taking place.'

'Oh, Gus, Gus!'

'What?'

'Jack was probably visiting the widder woman who's his lady-friend and who he's keeping quiet about in case Josephine learns about her. She doesn't like to share her brother with anyone, especially a widder woman who's free to marry again.'

'Oh!'

'So as you're wrong about all of them, you just let me know when you find someone else to suspect and I'll put you straight.' Detmeyer sighed. He looked suddenly very tired. 'Guess I've got you to thank for bringing me back home and saving my life.'

'Guess you have,' Greeley said with a grin. 'Ah, here comes your tasty beef tea. I'll leave you to enjoy it. And, Ann . . . '

'Miss Detmeyer to you,' growled her father.

'Miss Detmeyer, you make sure your father drinks it all.'

'I will.' Ann's eyes shone as she smiled at Greeley.

Detmeyer growled something else under his breath but neither of the other two took any notice.

'Where're you going, Gus? You ain't leaving my daughter here alone, I hope?' he asked more clearly.

'Of course I ain't. I'll stay till morning. Then I'm riding out again with Walsh. Try to find some trace of the killers. And rescue the two Baker girls.'

22

Dawn was just a streak in the eastern sky when the hut door opened and Claire and Rachel were shaken awake. Tired, afraid and hungry, they sat up to find the Mexican, Miguel, looming over them. Rachel shrank back but Claire refused to be intimidated, however much her heart beat with fear. She matched him stare for stare.

'My, but ain't you a feisty one!' Miguel said in his heavily accented voice. He chucked her under the chin, making her pull away and shake her head in disgust.

'Madame Rosa will like you. You will attract many customers once she has whipped you into shape. As for your sister, she will attract those who wish to hurt her.' He laughed crudely. 'And Madame Rosa is such that she will not stop them doing so. Now, little ladies, you must get up. Up you come.' He caught hold of Claire's arm and dragged her to her feet. 'It is time for you to leave here and travel to your new life in a Mexican bawdy-house. Should be fun. You will like it there.' He laughed again.

Claire loathed him more than ever. She had a good idea of what waited for her and Rachel in Mexico. *Fun* and *like* were not the words she'd use to describe it.

'Can't you just let us go?' Rachel whimpered, making the man laugh again. 'We won't say anything. We'll say it was Apaches took us.'

'Don't,' Claire told her. She took hold of one of her sister's hands, giving it a comforting squeeze. She wasn't about to beg for a mercy she knew would never be given. None of the men who'd taken them was in the least bit merciful.

They were pushed outside to where two of the men were eating breakfast. The girls knew the third one had gone into town to kill Marshal Detmeyer. He wasn't back yet and it gave Claire hope that not only had he not succeeded but that he had been caught in the attempt. She also hoped that her friend, Ann, hadn't been hurt.

'Sit down,' Nate ordered. 'Eat up.'

The young one, Bobby, gave them mugs of sludge-like coffee and plates of burnt bacon and beans; whatever sort of money they made from their outlawing they didn't eat or live well. The thought pleased Claire no end.

'Gotta fatten you up,' Miguel said. 'Mexicans don't like skinny white ass.' He pinched Rachel's arm, making her squeal with pain.

'Leave her alone,' Claire snapped.

The men smirked and Nate said, 'You're right, Miguel. She's a sassy one and no mistake.'

'Wish we could keep her with us,' Bobby said wistfully.

'Well we can't,' Nate told him. 'You heard what the boss said. He finds out we ain't killed 'em they'll be trouble for sure.'

Claire was relieved. If the men

decided to abuse them here and now there was no way she could stop them. On the way to Mexico with just Miguel accompanying them there might, *must*, be the chance to escape. Rescuers from Elk Horn must be looking for them, too, and maybe there would be someone who could follow whatever trail they took. If she did whatever she could to slow Miguel down and to leave clues behind to show where they were going, someone would surely catch up with them before they got to the border.

Miguel nodded. 'Anyway I'm 'bout ready to go. Get the ropes, Nate, and we'll be on our way.'

'Ropes?' Claire knew another spurt of fear. She glanced at Rachel, urging her not to give the men more satisfaction by crying or pleading. To her credit Rachel did neither, although she looked near to tears.

'That's right, lovely, ropes.' Nate grinned. He went over to the horses and brought back two short coils of rope. He seized Claire's hands and tied her wrists together in front of her. Tightly. So she couldn't prevent herself from gasping. He did the same to Rachel. The other ends of the ropes were tied to the saddle horn of Miguel's horse.

'You're making us walk?' Claire said in dismay. 'All that way?'

'Ain't that far,' Nate said. 'Will be hot and slow though.'

'Then why?'

'Cos, lovely, we ain't got a spare horse for you . . . '

Bobby muttered something about they would have had one had they taken the marshal's horse like Russ wanted and not left it behind. If the other men heard they took no notice.

' . . . and this way will make sure you don't try nothin' silly. Can't have you hoping you can escape.' Nate laughed to show how unlikely he thought their escape was. 'You're worth a helluva lot of money to us.'

'Get some of that starch outta you,

too,' Miguel said. In a fluid movement he mounted his horse. Nate reached up a hand to stop him.

'You are coming back, ain't you? With our share of the money?'

'Sure. Don't you trust me?' The man spoke as if his feelings were hurt by the accusation.

Nate said no more. The Mexican kept a sharp Bowie knife in his boot and he liked to use it.

Claire wondered whether he meant what he said. Certainly there didn't seem to be any love lost between the Mexican and the three white men. Once he'd crossed the border why should he bother to come all the way back here? He could stay with his precious Madame Rosa.

'Let's get going, little ladies. On our journey I will tell you all about what you can expect once you get to the bawdy-house. Might even show you, too. You at least.' He pointed at Claire.

Then he laughed so long and loudly that she made up her mind right there and then that she would do everything in her power to kill him.

'You believe him? That he will come back?' Bobby asked Nate as they watched Miguel ride away, the girls being pulled along behind him.

Nate shrugged. 'Who knows? But some of that money is ours and I ain't just letting him take it all. So we'll give him a few days and if he ain't back we'll head out the way he's gone. Follow him all the way to this Madame Rosa's if need be.'

Bobby could see all sorts of problems with that but he didn't say so. Nate didn't like anyone criticizing him.

'Anyway we daren't stay here much longer. Town's riled up, sure.'

Bobby said, 'The sooner we leave here the better. This whole thing ain't gone the way it should've.' He paused. He didn't want Nate accusing him of being a baby but he was worried. 'Russ oughtta be back by now.' He looked, not for the first time, at the trail that wound down the hillside. Still no sign of his brother. And it was fully light now. 'D'you think anything's happened to him?'

Nate hid his own worries. 'Nope. I bet Russ is warm and comfortable lying in a bed in the whorehouse. Where I'd like to be.'

'He was meant to come back straight away. He said he would.'

'Instead he obviously found a willing woman and decided she was better company. Can't say I blame him.'

'Mebbe.'

But Bobby wasn't convinced and as the minutes ticked away he became more and more worried. This wasn't like Russ. Russ was dependable and, having always looked out for his young brother, seldom did anything that he knew would worry him.

He spoke again. 'I hope he's OK Supposing he's hurt. Or fallen from his horse?'

Because Nate also thought that Russ's disappearance was unlike him, instead of telling Bobby to quit his whining, he slapped him on the shoulder.

'Tell you what,' he said, 'he ain't back in an hour or so we'll ride on down into Elk Horn and find out where he is.'

'The boss won't like that. He said we should stay away from the town.'

'Who cares about him? Who does he think he is, giving out his orders like he owns us? He don't. And I ain't scared of him.' Although he was; very. 'Anyway who's more important? The boss or your brother?'

Hearing it put like that, Bobby nodded.

'You're right. I'll go and saddle the horses so we're ready to ride.'

23

Greeley was just buckling on his gun when there was a knock on the door of the marshal's house. As the door was hanging off its hinges, he hoped it was someone coming to repair it. Instead it was a worried-looking Eddie Smith.

What now?

'What is it?'

Eddie stepped closer and said in a quiet voice,

'Melissa Fyfield is at the jailhouse. She's real upset and says she needs to see you urgently. But I couldn't very well let her come here, you know?'

Greeley did know. Marshal Detmeyer was a reasonably tolerant man. He knew towns like Elk Horn needed saloons and brothels; someplace where lonely men could enjoy a drink and the company of women. That didn't mean he would want a prostitute, even one like

Melissa, anywhere near his daughter.

'All right, I'll come with you,' he said. He called out a goodbye to Ann and then followed Eddie. 'She tell you what was wrong?'

The deputy shook his head. 'She didn't want to talk to me. She wanted you.'

Melissa was sitting at Eddie's desk. As soon as the two men went into the office, she jumped up and threw herself at Greeley, sobbing against his chest.

'What's the matter, sweetheart?' he asked. 'Has someone hurt you?' If so he'd see they were hurt back, no mistake about that.

'No, not me.' She gulped.

'But someone is hurt?'

'It's Roger. Two men attacked him last night and beat him up real bad.'

Greeley and Eddie exchanged a glance.

'They broke his fingers and . . . oh, Gus, it's awful.'

Greeley sat her back down in the chair. Eddie fetched her a mug of coffee, into which he poured some of the whiskey Detmeyer kept in his desk drawer for emergencies, of which this was surely one.

'I thought Roger was going to his room last night after I left you.'

'He was. He did.' Melissa nodded. 'But he usually goes for a walk before going to bed and so that's what he must've done last night.' She drank some of the coffee and wiped her eyes.

'Start at the beginning,' Greeley told her. 'Take your time.'

'Round about midnight Susie heard a great commotion under her window. She and Mr . . . well, her beau. I'd better not name names.'

Greeley smiled at her. 'Go on.'

'They got up and saw two men setting about another man. Susie realized it was Roger.'

'Did they see who his attackers were?' Greeley asked.

'No. It was too dark. But even though Mr . . . umm . . . yelled out to them to stop, they carried on hitting and kicking Roger. Mr . . . umm and Susie raised the alarm and several of us rushed to help.'

Despite there being nothing funny about the situation, Greeley couldn't help but smile to himself; that must have been a sight for sore eyes — all those girls and their clients in varying states of undress or no dress at all. Rushing outside into the cold night air.

'By the time we got downstairs and outside the two attackers had gone. Roger was lying on the ground.' Melissa started to cry again. 'He was covered in blood and was moaning. He looked terrible. I thought he was going to die.'

'But he didn't?'

'No.'

Greeley hugged her close. 'Your quick actions in going to help probably saved his life. What happened then?'

'Madame Josephine ordered us to bring him inside. Which some of the men did. After that they left, just in case their wives found out where they were. Me and Susie put Roger to bed and managed to persuade Josephine to call the doctor. She didn't want to at first, in case it cost her money, but even she had to admit how bad Roger was and that if he died on her premises it could cost her even more.' Melissa muttered something very rude about the woman under her breath.

'What did Doc say?'

'That Roger was lucky to be alive.' Tears threatened again. 'I can't believe anyone would do something like to Roger. He's such a nice man. Gentle, you know. Don't look down on us working girls.'

'I know, sweetheart. How is he this morning?'

'Still alive.'

'Is he awake?'

'He wasn't when I came to find you.'

'I'll come and see if he is now. He might know who did this to him.'

'Mr Greeley, do you think it's connected to the so-called Indian raid and the attack on Mr Detmeyer last night?'

Greeley turned to Eddie and frowned. 'I don't know. I don't really see how it could be, but just in case it is I want you to find a couple of men you can trust and ask them to stand guard at Sam's house. One in front. One at the back. I'm not about to take any chances.'

'Sure thing.'

'C'mon, Melissa, let's get you back to Josephine's before you're in trouble with her.'

'Mr Greeley,' Eddie called him back, 'I've just remembered. I was going to tell you. I got another telegram from Captain Harding.'

'What'd it say?'

'Just that his men had found no traces of the Baker girls. They've also buried Archie Ford.'

'Good. Anything else?'

'Yeah. Harding sent telegrams out to all the forts round about and messages have come back that there's been no sign of any Indian trouble anywhere. Just as he thought.'

'Send one back thanking him and asking him if he'll stand by if we should need help.'

Eddie nodded. 'Oh. One more thing. I'm sorry, Miss Fyfield, I know you're anxious to get back. But I've been looking through the Wanted posters to see if I can discover who it was you shot last night.'

'Any luck?'

'Not so far. I'll keep looking though.'

'Eddie, when did you last have anything to eat?'

'Er, yesterday, around noon. Had some crackers and soup later on.'

'You look real tired,' Melissa said, making him blush.

'Yeah, you do. So, Eddie, after you've arranged for guards at Sam's house, go on down to the café, have something to eat and drink and then get on home and rest up for a few hours. The Wanted posters can wait.'

'But there's no one to look after the office.'

'Ask someone from the courthouse to sit in here for a while. It won't do anyone any good if you make yourself ill over this.'

★ ★ ★

Greeley was shocked at the sight of Roger Keene. Not that he'd really thought Melissa was exaggerating, but she'd been so upset that he had wondered if the gambler could really be as bad as she said. Now he saw that she hadn't been exaggerating at all. He was worse if anything.

The man's face and what he could see of his body — chest, shoulders and arms — were a mass of cuts and purpling bruises. One eye was fully closed and the other swollen. Blood seeped from his broken nose. The fingers of both hands were smashed.

But he was still breathing and he was awake. As Greeley stepped closer to the bed, the poker player opened his swollen and bloodshot eye, just, and mumbled something. He also groaned with the agony his body was suffering. Melissa gripped Greeley's arm.

'Doc gave him something to help him sleep. It must be wearing off. What shall I do?'

'Best get him some whiskey. That'll

dull the pain at least. Is Hooper going to call again?'

'He said he would after he'd seen to his other patients.'

After he'd seen his respectable patients, Hooper had meant. Greeley pulled up a chair and sat close by the bed.

'Roger, I'm so sorry. Do you know who did this to you? Try and answer if you can. I know it hurts. Like hell.'

With a great effort Keene shook his head and, in between groans, said, 'Jumped me. Wearing masks.'

'You can't identify them?'

'No.'

'Gus, he really shouldn't ... ' Melissa began.

Greeley held out a hand to her. 'Just a couple of questions more. It's important. It might help identify his assailants.' He turned back to Keene. 'They say anything?'

'No.' A frown crossed Keene's face. 'Yes.'

'They did say something?'

A small nod. 'Leaving . . . '

'They were leaving because people were coming out of the brothel to help you?'

Nod.

'That's what they said? Something like 'let's get going'?'

'No.' Keene puffed a bit. 'Was going, but one came back to stamp on my hands. Said . . . That'll stop the sonofabitch cheating.' The gambler collapsed back on the pillow, exhausted, and closed his eyes. Greeley looked at Melissa.

'His fingers were deliberately broken in an effort to stop him playing cards.' A gambler needed nimble hands to shuffle the deck and deal the cards. A gambler with broken, misshapen fingers wouldn't be able to do so.

'How could they?' Melissa was horrified.

'Melissa, better get Roger that whiskey now. And, sweetheart, don't say a word about this to anyone. No one. Understand?'

She nodded.

24

As they rode out of Elk Horn Greeley told Walsh about the attack on Roger Keene.

'Who d'you think was responsible?'

'My best guess is the Preston brothers. There were two of the bastards, added to which was the talk of cheating. Most of the men Keene gambles with know he's an honest player and while they don't like losing money . . . ' Greeley shrugged, 'they also know that that goes with the game. Maybe Will is different and wants to win all the time. Or he simply resents losing money, and his brother encourages him. Will had accused Roger of cheating earlier in the evening.'

'You don't like 'em, do you?'

'Can't say I took to them, no. I think they're the ones behind the so-called Indian trouble, too, although I haven't got any evidence beyond a feeling in my gut.'

'Never ignore that. It's more likely them than Jack and Josephine. That pair wouldn't have the know-how or the daring to do something like that. And why should they do anything now anyway? They've talked before of leaving Elk Horn and going into farming. Ain't felt it necessary to stir up trouble to do so.'

'Sam says they've never got any further than talk anyway.'

'True.' Walsh was quiet for a little while, then he said, 'I can easily see the Preston boys thinking it would be a good idea to get people het up and laughing while others were killed.'

'You know something about them?' Greeley asked. 'You sound like you do.'

'Like you, not know for certain, no. But, Gus, I hear things. People come to Walter's saloon, they get drunk and they talk, and I listen. And a coupla bad things I've heard could well involve the Prestons.'

'What?'

'First off: a few weeks ago one of the very young doves, girl of no more'n fifteen who had a crib down by the river, left town all of a sudden. No word to anyone. Not even her so-called boyfriend who set her up there. He was hopping mad, I can tell you that.' Walsh grinned.

'Get on with it!'

'Seems that the night before Will Preston had paid her a visit. Up till then she'd seemed quite content, if not exactly happy, with what she was forced into doing.'

'Melissa said he came close to annoying one of the girls at the brothel one night when he was drunk,' said Gus, 'but Josephine threw him out before he could do anything.'

'Talk is he has a vile temper and wild manners. His brother is about the only thing that keeps him in check.'

'Yeah, heard that as well. More'n once. What else? You said there were two things.'

'One day the Prestons were riding through town. This was soon after they arrived. Three young boys set off firecrackers nearby, as kids sometimes do. Naughty, but boys are like that. Might not even have been meant to scare the Prestons. But their horses were scared all the same, and Will's reared and threw him into the muddy street. Boys laughed at him. He got real mad and frightened them real bad until David smoothed things over. Said it didn't matter. Later the boys' father apologized and that seemed to be that.'

'But it wasn't?'

'Mebbe not.' Walsh shrugged. 'A few days later the family home burnt down in the middle of the night. Real fierce fire, too. Everything gone. Luckily no one was hurt but that was only because the boys' dog barked and raised the alarm. Coulda all gone up in smoke otherwise.'

Greeley frowned. 'I spoke to Sam about the Prestons. As far as he knew they hadn't caused any trouble.'

'Detmeyer can't be everywhere and he ain't told everything as goes on in the town. You know that. Anyhow, the fire was thought to be an accident. How would the marshal know any different? Dry night, high winds, a casually tossed away match. These things happen all the time.'

'You don't think it was an accident though?'

'Don't remember thinking anything much at the time. Wasn't nothing to do with me. Now, I wonder. And, Gus, if we're right about 'em and they find out we suspect 'em, then we'd better watch our backs, don't you think?'

Greeley nodded. Yes, he did.

25

'What the hell is going on over there?' Bobby indicated the large and excited crowd gathered in front of the undertaker's.

They were looking at something displayed in the window and were talking and gesticulating to one another.

'Nate, what is it?' He suddenly sounded frightened.

Nate glanced at him. He had a dreadful feeling that he knew what — who — the men, women and children found so fascinating. If he was right Bobby was sure as hell not going to be happy. Nor was he, come to that.

'We'd best go and see,' he said.

The two young men dismounted and tied their horses' reins to the nearest hitching rail. They pushed their way into the crowd, filled with a foreboding that increased with every step.

'Oh hell, no!' Bobby cried in horror. He would have collapsed but for Nate's grabbing his arm.

For there, in pride of place in the centre of the undertaker's window, displayed in a coffin, was the dead body of his brother, Russ. In front of it was a sign. As neither of the two could read, Bobby asked the man nearest them to read it out. It said:

A coward shot to death while trying to kill Marshal Detmeyer. Does anyone know who he is? Reward of $10 for information.

'The bastards not only killed him, now they're trying to make money out of him.' Bobby began to shiver, his eyes were wet with unshed tears.

'Hush.' Nate was aware of several men glancing their way. Their looks weren't particularly friendly.

'You know the bastard?' demanded someone close by, poking Nate in the ribs.

'No.'

'Sounds like you do.'

'Well we don't. C'mon, Bobby, this ain't nothing to do with us.' Nate pulled the younger man back towards their horses.

'But — '

'We can't do nothing for Russ. Not now. We act suspicious in front of them,' Nate nodded towards the crowd, 'we'll be arrested for sure. Russ wouldn't want that so for chrissakes pull yourself together.'

Bobby stood his ground. 'That's my brother over there on display. Shot dead. Someone's gotta pay.'

'I know and I'm sorry but, Bobby, we've gotta think of ourselves.'

But Bobby couldn't think of anything but his brother.

'I'm goin' to ask Preston what happened.'

Nate sighed. 'That might not be a good idea.'

'I don't care if it is or isn't. I want to know — I must know — what happened to Russ. You don't have to come with me.'

'No, I'll go with you. Then we leave Elk Horn for good.'

Nate was scared that if they hung around town too long people might connect both of them to Russ and the attack on the Baker farm. They'd be hanged for sure, with people baying for their blood as they were led out to the gallows. He regretted more than anything becoming involved with David and Will Preston. Miguel had warned him that they were dangerous men and that it could be very dangerous to agree to do what they wanted, but he hadn't listened; he'd listened instead to the chink of Preston's money.

* * *

Miguel whistled tunelessly as he rode along. Every once in a while he looked back at his captives. Leered at them. Laughed. Especially at the younger one who was oh so clearly terrified of him.

In order to confirm who was in charge he pulled on the ropes if they showed any sign whatsoever of not keeping up. But he'd decided that whenever he stopped to rest himself and his horse, he would allow them a drink from his canteen; he didn't want them fainting or falling ill. Not too much though, because neither did he want them to think he was about to treat them kindly.

In the same way, when they stopped for the night he'd give them something to eat. Madame Rosa wouldn't want to buy two bags of bones from him.

'How are my little ladies doing?' he asked over his shoulder. 'Not going too fast, am I?'

'Don't worry about us,' Claire said. 'We're not in any hurry to get where you're taking us.'

Miguel laughed. 'You will not have to walk much further, little ladies. By tomorrow I will have tamed you so well I'll be able to let you ride on the horse with me.'

'In your dreams,' Claire muttered.

He laughed again. He had determined that after eating supper he was going to take one of them to bed. As he couldn't decide which — the feisty one would be more fun but then it would be nice to hurt the scared one and make her even more scared — he'd probably take them both.

He couldn't understand why he hadn't been allowed to bed them before this. That's what little white girls were for. He didn't understand either why Nate and the other two hadn't also taken advantage of the situation. Why take the girls along in the first place if you didn't mean to use them? But then there was a helluva lot he didn't understand about white men in general and those three in particular.

Of course, he had no intention whatsoever of returning to them with the money he got from Madame Rosa. Not that bunch of idiots! He was fed up with them, their whining, their uselessness and their company. He regretted meeting them and agreeing to join their so-called gang. Gang? Nate was full of big words and bragging but his deeds didn't match up, so they'd not only nearly been caught by the law several times but, even worse, had hardly made enough from their robberies and raids to buy food and drink, let alone enjoy the luxury of a night in a fancy whorehouse. That was until this deal with the Preston brothers had come along. Preston said it would make them a fortune and secure their reputations as real bad men. Did he know how to sweet-talk them!

Instead . . . what a deal it had turned out to be. Pretending to be Apaches, firing bows and arrows, whooping. Acting like a bunch of kids. Killing a farmer and his family and frightening cowboys.

The others were so greedy that they did whatever David Preston ordered. They fawned over him, agreed to whatever he said, not just because they wanted paying but really because they were shit-scared of him. Especially after he said he was wanted back in Kansas and Missouri for killing anyone who got in his way.

Did Miguel believe him? Yes. You could see the man's ruthlessness in his eyes. As for his brother, Will, what a madman he was.

It didn't matter. Miguel was going to stay in Mexico for a while at least. Strike out on his own. Perhaps he'd stick with Madame Rosa for a month or more. She was old enough to be his mother and ugly with it, but she still knew a thing or two about keeping a man happy.

In the meantime there were his two little ladies to enjoy. He couldn't wait for night-time. In fact, why wait? He was his own man now, beholden to no one. He could do whatever he wanted. Whenever he wanted.

'We will stop soon, little ladies,' he called back to Claire and Rachel. 'You see those trees and rocks up ahead. They mean a water hole. It will be a pleasant spot and there you will both make me a very happy man. Very happy indeed.'

'Not if I can help it,' Claire muttered through gritted teeth.

'What does he mean?' Rachel asked.

'Nothing. Don't worry.'

Claire must be ready, she was ready, to do whatever it took to stop him. She would not allow him to hurt Rachel. She wouldn't.

26

David Preston was not in the least bit pleased when he opened the front door and saw Nate and Bobby standing on the porch.

'What the hell are you two doing here?' He grabbed hold of them, pulling them inside. He peered out. Thank God no one was around to see.

'Who is it?' Will asked, coming into the hallway, bottle of whiskey in his hand. 'Oh, it's you.'

'I thought I warned you never to come here,' David said angrily, pushing at Nate. 'That we shouldn't be seen together.'

'Hell, boss, I'm sorry but — '

Bobby, all fear of the two brothers gone in his grief, stepped forward, cutting Nate short.

'What happened to Russ? How come he's on display for all to see in the undertaker's? Shot. Dead. He was my brother.'

Will smirked. 'Stupid idiot couldn't even kill an old wounded man lying asleep in bed. How hard could that be? Instead he botched it up completely. He asked for trouble.'

'How dare you!' Bobby yelled. 'If the job was so damn simple why didn't you kill the marshal yourself? No, you get us to do all your dirty work while you keep outta sight.'

'I went out raiding with you,' Will said. 'Good fun that was, too.'

'We paid you well,' David Preston said. 'It's not our fault Russ didn't do the job properly and got caught.'

'All the money in the world ain't worth Russ's life,' shouted Bobby.

'We sure didn't sign up for this,' Nate added, getting back some of his bravado. 'Russ was a good man.'

'Oh, get a grip,' Will said, taking a swig out of the bottle. 'He was a cheapskate outlaw the same as you two. You become an outlaw you know the

215

risks you run. The way you lot go about your business it's a wonder you ain't all been killed long before this.'

'Who shot him?' Bobby demanded. He looked as if he'd like to punch Will but, knowing his reputation, didn't quite dare.

'Some damn bounty hunter name of Greeley,' the elder Preston said. 'Been hanging around town for a while now, interfering in things that shouldn't concern him.'

'Bastard should ride out after more bounties, not try to stop our plans,' Will put in. 'We'll deal with him good and proper before too long. Despite the reputation he's got. We're better'n him. Him and that no good Injun-lover he's so friendly with.'

'I'll kill him myself.'

David Preston laughed and patted Bobby's shoulder.

'There, there, shouldn't try iffen I was you. He's cleverer, faster on the draw and a better shot than you'll ever be. No, sonny, best leave us grown-ups to deal with him. After we've sorted out this problem.'

'What d'you mean?' Nate demanded.

'Just that despite what Will says and, although in some ways he's right, we've got to see to you fair and square.'

Nate looked pleased. That sounded like only one thing: more money!

'You kill them girls like I ordered you to?'

'Sure thing, Mr Preston.'

'Why do I get the feeling you're not telling me the truth?'

'It is the truth.'

'You're not a very good liar, son. Where's that Mexican? Where's he? He around?'

'He left us.'

'Why?'

'He's going back to Mexico. Don't worry, we can do without him.'

'Don't know why you were running with a Mexican in the first place,' Will said with an ugly sneer.

'He was OK at first.' Nate paused before adding, 'Mr Preston, d'you want us to do any more for you?'

'Nate!' Bobby cried. 'No! Russ is dead because of them. We can't work for them any more.'

'He's dead because of his own stupid fault.' Will said with a sneer. 'He deserved to get shot.'

'You bastard!' Bobby launched himself at Will.

Although Will was momentarily taken by surprise by the sudden, unexpected attack, he was quickly more than a match for the younger man: stronger, more ruthless. Bobby didn't stand a chance against him.

They went down on to the floor in a blur of arms and legs. Quickly Will head-butted Bobby and scrambled to his feet. Bobby cried out in pain and blood streamed from his broken nose. Will kicked him several times, hard, in the ribs, in the stomach.

'Hey, stop that!' Nate yelled.

David Preston caught hold of his arm, preventing him from going to help his friend.

'He started it. Let Will finish it.'

Finish it Will did. Speedily and without any more fuss. He pulled an almost unconscious Bobby to his feet, drew a knife from his belt and stuck it hard and deep into Bobby's chest. The young man let out one awful scream before flopping to the floor, his eyes glazing over even as he fell.

'Jesus Christ!' Nate cried out, jumping out of the way. His hand went towards his gun.

He never made it.

Will threw his knife, handle first, to his brother, who caught it one-handed. With his other hand he flung Nate round and, seizing his hair, pulled his head back. Before Nate could do anything Preston had slit his throat from one ear to the other, leaving behind a deep and bloody gash. Nate grabbed at his throat, making some horrible gurgling noises, before collapsing beside Bobby.

Some of the blood had splashed on to Will and now he began to laugh, bouncing from one foot to the other.

'That showed 'em! Idiots!'

He surely did like killing people.

'Certainly saves paying them.' Preston looked down at the two bodies, no feeling in his face or voice. It was their fault entirely for coming to the house and making a needless fuss. He was pleased to be rid of them. They hadn't carried out his orders properly and he was sure they hadn't killed the girls.

When he'd calmed down a bit, Will said,

'What shall we do with these silly bastards?'

'We'll put them out back till it gets dark, then we'll take them to the river and throw them in. About all they're good for. No one will connect them with us. We're so respectable. I want to keep it that way. For now anyway.'

Will giggled.

'So while I clean up the mess and blood in here,' continued his brother, 'I want you to ride out to the hideout and make sure there's nothing left there that could implicate us.'

'Sure thing.'

'And if you find that these two,' Preston indicated the bodies, 'have lied to us and the girls are still alive, then you know what you have to do, don't you?'

'Absolutely.' Will fingered his knife.

'Same with the Mexican.'

'I hope he isn't dead. I'll enjoy dealing with him. What if they ain't there?'

Preston thought for a minute or two.

'Follow them. I don't want any witnesses left behind who may be able to identify us.'

'OK,' Will agreed cheerfully.

27

Along the way to the Baker farm, Walsh said,

'Tell you what, Gus, rather than spend valuable time riding up and down the riverbank trying to find the raiders' tracks, which could take a while, why don't we head for the spot where those two idiot cowboys were shot at?'

'That's right at the head of Five-Mile Valley,' Greeley objected. 'Could be taking us well out of our way. It'll take time too.'

'But the bastards might not have been so careful there.'

'Why not?'

'One thing, it was night. They couldn't see if they were leaving any trail behind or not. No river that way for 'em to ride into. They might've been so pleased with themselves over the

Baker raid that they got careless. I reckon that's our best chance of finding something easily.'

'Worth a try, I guess.' Greeley didn't sound too sure.

'And if we don't find anything we can head back for the river and try there.'

The place where Pete and Mike had been attacked was at the very end of the valley, where a steep and rocky hill overlooked a wide, grassy meadow. Cows still grazed there overseen by two cowboys, who had rifles out and laid across their saddles, ready for trouble. Greeley waved to them indicating they meant no harm, but the cowboys continued to watch them, taking no chances.

Walsh dismounted and handed the reins of his horse to Greeley.

'Yeah, this is where the attack took place. Ground is all churned up.'

'Is it the same horses?'

Walsh grinned. 'Sorry, Gus, even I ain't that good a tracker. I can't tell one horse's hoofs from another unless there's something distinctive about 'em. Only two horses, though. Tracks heading off in that direction.' He pointed up the valley. 'The riders sure ain't taking too much care about whether they've left a trail behind. They're making it easy for us to follow 'em. I hoped they might but it's still strange when they were so careful after hitting the Baker farm.'

Greeley pondered that.

'Maybe on that occasion they were told to be careful. Maybe this time they weren't given orders or they didn't think taking precautions would be necessary. They probably aren't blessed with many brains.'

Not long after this conversation they came to a meadow that sloped gently up between trees and rocks. There at the top was a line shack and a corral of sorts.

'That's the way they rode,' Walsh said. 'Reckon that shack'd make a good hideout, don't you? Clear view all round. Miles from anywhere. Only trouble is it don't look like anyone is there now. The corral is empty.'

Greeley nodded. 'Even so, Henry, let's go real easy. You're probably right but if the men are still here we don't want to spook them into doing anything hasty. Especially if that puts the girls in harm's way. I don't want them getting hurt by any actions of ours.'

'We also want to take the bastards alive if possible.' Walsh knew Greeley's reputation. 'That way they can confess out loud in a court of law that it was them and not Apaches who killed the Bakers. I think there are still a lot of people in Elk Horn need to be told that loud and clear.'

'And we need to know for sure who hired them. They want catching as well.'

The two men rode as quietly as possible up the slope, keeping to the edge of the trees and out of sight of any watchers. But it was quickly obvious that no one was about.

'Damn!' Greeley muttered.

He was worried. Were they going to find the bodies of the Baker girls? His eyes raked the scene. He could see no sign of any freshly dug graves, but then, if the men had killed their captives it was hardly likely they would stay around to bury them.

'Whoever was here hasn't been gone long.' Walsh indicated the remains of a campfire in front of the shack.

'If only we'd been quicker we'd've caught the bastards.'

'Looks like they mean to come back. Unless they just left their plates and mugs behind, which ain't likely.'

'Wonder where they've gone?'

They dismounted by the corral. Greeley took a deep breath and went into the shack. He let it out when he realized the girls' bodies weren't there. But while he was thankful for that he was disappointed because, if the men were going to return to the hideout, he'd hoped they would have left Claire and Rachel behind. Now it seemed the girls had been taken along, although he couldn't really figure out why.

'Where are they?' he cried in frustration. 'What's happened to them?'

'They were here,' Walsh said. 'Look.' He picked up a lace handkerchief lying on the floor.

Greeley went outside, pacing up and down. He didn't really know what to do. Perhaps they could lie in wait for the men and take them by surprise. Capture them. But if Walsh was wrong and they had gone for good, then to stay here would be a waste of time.

'Water the horses, Gus. I'll see what I can find.'

Soon Walsh hurried back, a worried look on his face.

'I've found two sets of tracks heading in two different directions.'

'They've split up?'

'One is a man on horseback and he's leading two others who are on foot.'

Claire and Rachel!

'Oh, hell!'

'They're heading that way. Towards Mexico.'

'Why there?'

'Think about it. The girls are probably being taken to a Mexican brothel.'

'What?' Greeley was horrified. 'But they're only kids.'

Walsh laughed. 'Where you been, son? They're young and fresh. Just what whorehouses like. Bet your Melissa wasn't much older than them when she started out.'

Greeley nodded. The thought didn't give him any comfort. It just made him sad for Melissa.

'Trouble is, brothels in Mexico make Josephine's place and the way she treats her girls seem like a palace. And white girls will be treated even worse than Mexican señoritas or Indian squaws.'

Greeley swore several times. He wanted nothing more than to get his hands on the sons-of-bitches responsible and wring their necks.

'They left early today. Tracks are fresh.'

'We've gotta get after them. They can't have gone far. We can catch them up before they get anywhere near the border.'

'Wait up.' Walsh caught hold of his arm. 'The other tracks are of two horses and they're heading towards Elk Horn.'

Greeley came to a halt.

'God! You think they're after Sam again? Ann could be hurt.' Men were guarding the Detmeyer's house but they might not be expecting any more trouble, might not take too much care. Yet there were the Baker girls to consider.

Walsh realized Gus's dilemma.

'Don't worry,' he said. 'You go on back to town. Help the marshal and his daughter.'

'What about you?'

'I'll go after the girls.'

28

'Keep following the meadow down and you'll come to the river,' Walsh said. 'Follow that into Elk Horn. Won't take you long.'

'OK Good luck.'

'You too. I'll see you soon.'

Greeley kicked his horse into a steady lope. He glanced back once over his shoulder but the scout was already lost to view. He hoped Walsh would find the girls and be able to rescue them, and he hoped he'd reach town before any harm could come to Sam or Ann.

As he rode along he thought back over all that had happened and wondered if he should have done anything different. Maybe left it to Captain Harding and the army, or enlisted more men to help him. But he'd done what he considered right at the time and it was too late to change it now.

What was that noise?

★   ★   ★

Will Prescott collected his horse from the livery stable and rode quickly out of town. Once he was alone, he laughed out loud and yelled in delight.

Killing those two idiots had been great fun — the looks on their faces when they knew they were about to die! Just like the fun he'd had on the raid of the Baker farm. The look on that woman's face when she realized her husband and son were dead had been even better. Pity she hadn't lived long enough to know they'd found her two daughters. It would have been good to hear her plead and beg for them to be let go. There would be more fun tonight when he and David threw the idiots in the river. Good riddance.

The only pity lately had been that they were interrupted before they could hurt that damn cheat of a gambler some more. Still, at least the sonofa-bitch wouldn't be able to play for a long, long while. Serve him right.

Will laughed again.

Kansas had been getting dangerous, with the law closing in on them, but he hadn't wanted to leave. Now he admitted that coming to Arizona and Elk Horn was just about the best thing he and David had ever done. The beauty of it was that no one suspected them. They could wreak all sorts of mischief and get away with it.

★ ★ ★

'Papa! Just what do you think you're doing?' Ann had gone into Detmeyer's room with more beef tea only to find her father out of bed and getting dressed. 'Get back into bed this instant!'

'I'm sorry, sweetheart, but I can't.' Detmeyer gave her a smile that she didn't return. Instead she was stony-faced. 'I've got to go on down to the office.'

'Whatever for? Don't be silly.'

'With all that's going on I can't leave Eddie alone any longer to cope by himself.'

'He's been managing all right up till now.'

'He's on his own. He has been for several days. It ain't fair.'

'But you're not well enough.'

Detmeyer took hold of Ann by the shoulders.

'I can't stay in bed a moment longer, I really can't. I'll go crazy. I feel much better, honestly. Look, I promise not to do anything except sit in the office while Eddie brings me up to date and then goes home for a rest. That's all.'

'I'm not sure I believe you.' Ann knew her father only too well. 'Supposing something happens while Eddie's not there, you'll want to go and sort it out.'

'No, I won't.'

'Yes you will, and so that's why I'm going with you, to make sure that you behave yourself.'

'I refuse to let you.' Detmeyer looked shocked. 'The marshal's office is no place for a young lady.'

'I don't see why not. You'll be there to shield me. If you don't let me go with you, I won't let you go.' Ann could be as stubborn as her father.

He recognized the look on her face. She wasn't going to listen to reason any more than he was.

'OK but only if you make a promise as well.'

'What is it?'

'To keep out of trouble.'

'You will, I will. And while I get ready you can enjoy your beef tea. It's nice and hot. Don't let it get cold.'

Detmeyer groaned. Once he was at the office he had been going to send Eddie out for a plate of good food — beef and potatoes and squash — from the café, as well as a full bottle of whiskey from The Antlers. That was out of the question now.

★ ★ ★

234

David Preston returned from flinging the dead bodies of Nate and Bobby into the yard out back and went to the window. He wasn't sure he liked the way things were going. He'd wanted to start afresh here. Buy land and cows and become a successful and wealthy rancher, respectable and law-abiding. So far it hadn't worked out that way. Maybe with Will by his side it never would, although it was hardly their fault they'd been forced into violence and killing. They might have to move on again.

Ah! That was surprising. Detmeyer was walking by, leaning heavily on the arm of his daughter, who didn't look very happy. He was wearing his marshal's badge. Despite being wounded he must be heading for the office.

If so then that gave Preston the perfect opportunity to visit him and, by pretending to be concerned for the man's health and the whole situation — even offering his help, find out exactly what Detmeyer remembered about the Baker raid. Deal with him if necessary — and not make a hash of it, either. It was best never to rely on others; he should have learnt that lesson by now. He'd wait until Will got back and they could go together.

Concerned citizens!

* * *

Will was almost halfway to the hideout when he caught a glimpse of a rider coming down the hill through the trees. Whoever it was he was too far away for Will to make out. And he hadn't spotted him either. Who would be out here, where there was nothing for miles around? Why? Perhaps it was Miguel coming to look for his friends. If so, he could do what David wanted and shoot the Mexican from ambush. He'd shoot the rider anyway. Serve the idiot right for being where he shouldn't be.

Will guided his horse into the shade of the trees and dismounted. He pulled his rifle from its scabbard and waited.

Before long he recognized the man coming towards him.

It was Gustavus Greeley: bounty hunter and all round damn nuisance! He was riding all unknowing right into a trap! Talk about Will's lucky day!

He raised his rifle and fired!

29

'Here we are, little ladies,' Miguel said with a smirk and a chuckle. 'Was I not right? Is this not a pleasant spot for us to spend some time getting to know one another really, really well?'

He rode his horse into the shade of the cottonwood trees growing by the side of a small water hole and dismounted. Grinning, he untied the ropes from his saddle horn, freeing Claire and Rachel.

'Can't you untie our wrists as well? Please?' Claire said. 'What harm can we do you out here?'

'Do not be silly, little lady. I have seen the way you stare at me. You do not like me, I know. But I am all heart. You can rest now. For a while anyway.'

Rachel immediately sank to the dusty ground. Claire crouched beside her. She stared defiantly up at the Mexican, even while her stomach twisted with fear.

'You've made us walk so far,' she said. 'My sister is worn out. Our feet are covered in blisters and we are both sunburnt.'

'Do not worry.' Miguel came over and looked down at his captives, chuckling. 'We will not be moving from here for the rest of the day and the night. Soon, as I said, you will be mine completely and you will ride with me at least for some of the way.'

'Is that meant to make us feel better?'

'It's meant to make you feel grateful.' Miguel's voice rose to a shout and for a moment Claire feared he would hit her. 'I do not have to do this for you. So enough! You are here to serve me, not to argue. So you,' he pointed at Rachel, 'instead of resting, you help me gather up some brush for a fire. Blame your stubborn sister and her attitude towards me for that. And while you do, she can think about how she had better start being nice to me. I can make your lives an utter misery. If you are good it will be a little easier. For now we will build a fire. Have some coffee and biscuits. Then we will see what happens.'

He dragged Rachel up by her hair, making her squeal with pain, and shoved her towards the water hole.

As soon as his back was to her Claire began to tug at the ropes binding her wrists. *Please, Rachel*, she thought, *take your time in finding enough brush. Keep him occupied.*

But after a few moments she realized that she would never have enough time to free her hands. The rope was too tough and the knots too tight. All she was succeeding in doing was chafing her wrists and making them bleed.

Not willing to give up, she glanced round. The ground beneath the cotton-woods was littered here and there with stones. Maybe one of them would be nice and sharp. Miguel was on the far side of the water hole, enjoying himself too much in tormenting Rachel to take any notice of his other captive.

The stone Claire found was small but it had a jagged edge. Awkwardly she picked it up between finger and thumb and began to rub at the ropes. Was it working? *Yes! Oh, please, yes.* Surely the ropes had started to fray?

Damn! Miguel was coming back. Quickly she sat down again, pretending she hadn't moved. The ropes definitely felt easier. She could work them loose and free her hands.

Then what? Miguel's horse. His rifle was still in its scabbard. He was so sure of himself and his hold over them, so sure they were too scared of him to try to escape, that he was getting careless. The rifle seemed her best hope as she doubted she could find a way to get hold of either his revolver or his knife, both of which he kept on his person. Could she get it without him seeing her?

'Ah, little lady, I see you have decided to be a good girl,' Miguel said, at the same time giving Rachel a push that sent her sprawling. 'It is the only way. I will be nice to you if you are very nice to me. So smile for me, or maybe I will hurt this other little one and you wouldn't like that.' He kicked Rachel hard, before pulling her to her feet.

Claire gritted her teeth and, hoping she sounded nice, said,

'Where are the coffee and biscuits? Are they in your saddle-bags?' *Where the rifle is.* 'I'll get them while, Rachel, you start the fire.' She got to her feet, hoping that Miguel was fooled by her act.

He wasn't.

'A good offer my little one but I have now changed my mind. I do not trust you or your sudden change of heart. So first, before anything else, you must learn to obey me in every way and not even allow yourself to think of not doing so. Become mine. Besides, I cannot wait. So I have decided to enjoy myself with one of you. Which of my pretty little ladies is to be?'

Rachel gave a little cry of horror and tried to shrink behind Claire.

242

Claire knew that he would choose Rachel. He would not only take delight in frightening the already terrified girl even more, but he wanted to punish Claire by making her watch. Did he really believe that that would make her only too willing to do whatever he wanted? If so he was sadly mistaken. She didn't bother to argue or plead with him. Instead she said, 'You bastard. I'll never give in to you. I'll see you in hell first.'

Swearing, Miguel hit her round the jaw and then shoved her aside so hard that she fell over, landing with a painful bump.

'Stop it!' Rachel cried. 'Leave her be.'

Swearing some more about impossible females, he strode over to Rachel, grabbed hold of her, pulled her towards him. She started to scream and struggle. Miguel pawed at her, trying to kiss her, laughing as he did so.

Claire pulled on the ropes as hard as she could, twisting her hands this way and that, not caring that her wrists were being torn to shreds. *At last!* One hand was free! She ran for the horse: pulled the rifle from its scabbard. It was much heavier than she expected and she almost dropped it. Then she suddenly realized that she had never fired a gun before. Her father had been strict about such things and said that shooting wasn't something young girls did.

Now if she fired at Miguel the bullet might miss him altogether. What on earth would he do to her then for trying to kill him? Even worse, she might hit Rachel instead.

There had to be another way . . .

Miguel had pushed Rachel to the ground, was fumbling with her clothes. Now, when he was occupied, was her chance. She ran up behind the man and swung the rifle with all her might at his head. Crack! He howled in pain and collapsed.

'Let's go!' Rachel cried. She scrambled up. Her face was wet with tears and her eyes full of fear.

'No, not yet.'

Why not?'

'He's still alive.' He could still come after them. Was even now opening his eyes and groaning. He still posed a threat. Somehow he sat up, holding his head. 'What you do that for?' he slurred. 'You naughty lady. I punich you both.'

'I don't think so.' Claire pointed the barrel of the rifle at him, pleased and proud that her hands were steady. 'Rachel, get behind me.'

Miguel laughed. 'Do not be so silly, little lady. It's not loaded.' He attempted to get to his feet and fell back down again.

'Claire?'

For a moment Claire felt as dismayed as her sister sounded. She thought about hitting Miguel again but, even though he was hurt, if she got too close to him he might yet be strong enough to grab the rifle away from her.

But was he telling the truth? She couldn't believe he would have an unloaded weapon with him. It didn't make sense. Supposing they had encountered dangers — either

man or animal — he would have wante
to be ready, not waste time loading hi.
rifle. It wasn't as if he'd kept it unloaded
because he thought his 'little ladies' would
cause any trouble.

'We'll see, shall we?' She knew she
was right as fear came into the man's
eyes.

'Give the gun to me!' he screamed.

She pulled the trigger. The recoil
knocked her over, but at that close
range even she couldn't miss. The bullet
struck Miguel in the chest. He fell back,
his feet kicked once or twice, then he
lay still.

Cautiously, the rifle held ready to fire
again, Claire got up. She went towards
him.

'What are you doing?' Rachel asked.

'Making sure the bastard is dead.'

30

Greeley saw the flash of the rifle before he heard the shot. That saved his life.

In that same instant he dived off his horse. Just in time. The sound of the shot reached him even as the bullet whooshed the air above him and ploughed harmlessly into the ground. His horse whinnied in fright and might have run away, but somehow Greeley managed to hold on to the reins.

There was another shot. That was even closer.

Quickly he pulled the horse back towards the tree line, grabbing at his own rifle as he did so. His assailant was in the trees almost at the bottom of the hill. Greeley couldn't see him but the flash of the rifle gave away his position. He flung himself on to the ground and, lying prone, sent several shots of his own in the man's direction.

★ ★ ★

Damn! This wasn't going the way it should. The bounty hunter should be dead. Obviously he was as good as his reputation. Wily. Fast on the trigger. Not as good as David, who was completely ruthless and fearless, but good enough to make Will scared that if he stayed where he was he might be hit.

Will liked killing people. He didn't like the thought of being killed. Best to run and fight another day was his motto. He sent two more shots at Greeley, then jumped to his feet and mounted his horse in one swift movement. He spurred it into a gallop.

Greeley realized that his assailant was getting away. There he went! Still Greeley couldn't make him out clearly enough to identify him: he was too far away for that. His horse was nondescript as well. But surely the attack was connected with the rest of what was going on. The man might even be one of the gang who'd raided the Baker

.m. Who else would be out here so
ear to the hideout?

Greeley leapt on his horse and
started after the man.

It was no good.

They traded a few more shots but the
man had too much of a head start for
Gus to catch up. Before long the other
animal and its rider had disappeared
from view amongst the trees that led
eventually to the river. There was no
point in continuing the chase, especially
as he could easily be riding into another
ambush. Cursing, he pulled his horse to
a halt and patted its neck, soothing it.

After a while Will realized he was in
the clear. He laughed; he'd outwitted
the bounty hunter. He'd known that he
would! All the same it would be best
not to mention any of this to David. His
brother didn't like anyone who failed to
carry out his orders. He'd be angry that
Will had taken it upon himself to try
and shoot Greeley and, worse, had
committed the ultimate sin by not
succeeding. He'd be even angrier that

Will had never made it to the hideou

Best to pretend that he had; best to say that no one and nothing was there and hope that that was true.

★   ★   ★

Walsh had no difficulty in following the trail: a horse and two people on foot, the rider making no effort to hide the tracks. They were also travelling slowly. How could it be otherwise with two girls having to walk? Besides, as they were heading for Mexico there really was only one route they could take that would provide water and grass. He'd catch up by nightfall, maybe sooner.

He wondered what to do when he did. He had no qualms whatsoever about killing the bastard who was taking two young girls to a life of servitude in Mexico, after shooting their family. He'd even have no qualms either about shooting him in the back or when he was asleep. Walsh was not a man to worry about playing fair with an utlaw. At the same time he'd quite like to take whoever it was back to Elk Horn to face trial and the hangman.

By far the most important thing was that he wanted to save the girls and not get them hurt.

Suddenly he stopped.

His still sharp ears had picked up the sound of a distant gunshot. A rifle. He knew there was a small water hole up ahead. Don't say whoever was taking the girls to Mexico had decided they were too much of a nuisance and had shot them instead. Not when he was so close to rescuing them. Or had they run into some sort of trouble? There were no further shots and he didn't know what that meant.

He kicked his horse into a gallop.

He hadn't gone far when he spotted a horse being ridden towards him. His eyes, like his ears, were still sharp and he realized that it was being ridden by two girls.

'Hey! Hey!' he yelled and waved his arms in the air to attract their attention.

'Who's that?' Rachel said fearfull
'It's not one of the others, is it?'

'I'll shoot him too if it is.' Claire's
heart beat fast. Please, oh please, don't
say they'd made their escape only to be
caught again.

The rider came closer, slowly, hands
out in front of him to show he wasn't
reaching for a weapon. He was an old
man with long grey hair, riding a pinto
pony. Claire had never seen him before
and he certainly wasn't one of the gang.
In fact, he looked a bit like an Indian
from the way he was dressed but he
wasn't that either. Who was he? Friend
or foe?

Walsh stopped as he neared the two
girls who had also come to a halt. He
dismounted.

'I don't mean you no harm,' he
called. After all they'd been through,
how to reassure them that that was
true? 'I'm from Elk Horn. Are you
Claire and Rachel Baker? Friends of
Ann Detmeyer? She's very worried
about you. We all are. I'm here to take

ou back to town and back to her and our other friends.'

'Oh!' Rachel sobbed in relief. Before Claire could stop her she slid off the horse and ran towards the man. She flung herself into his arms, weeping against his chest.

'It's OK,' he said, patting her back. 'All right. You're safe now. Both of you.' He held out a hand to Claire and she dismounted, still holding on to the rifle, still wary, not yet willing to believe that they were indeed safe.

'Who are you?' she demanded.

'My name is Henry Walsh. I live in Elk Horn. I've been helping people look for you. Are you hurt? Did anyone hurt you?'

'They killed our family,' Rachel cried. 'They killed Mama and Papa and our brother, Frank.'

'I know, sweetheart.'

'And they took us captive. We were so scared. We thought they would kill us too. It was so frightening.'

'Did they hurt you?' Walsh repeated

his earlier question.

'No.' Claire shook her head, knowing what he meant. 'How did you find us?'

Walsh knew the girl was suspicious of him; he didn't blame her.

'Me and Gustavus Greeley — do you know who he is? He's a friend of Ann and the marshal. Anyway the two of us found the hideout the gang was using. Once I was a scout for the army and I followed your tracks. I thought I might catch up with you at the water hole. What happened? How did you get away?'

'Claire shot Miguel.'

Walsh looked at the girl in admiration.

'That was brave of you. He dead?'

'Yes. I think so.'

'I'd best go and make sure.'

'There's no need. After I shot him we tied his hands and feet up. Real good and tight. And we took his knife away so he couldn't get free.'

Walsh grinned. If this Miguel wasn't dead he soon would be, out here in the esert, wounded, with no way of getting untied and no horse to ride away on. A man on foot would never last long in the desert; even one who hadn't been shot. He didn't want to take chances but he didn't want to waste any more time either. Best to get these two girls back to town.

'Don't go. Don't leave us,' Rachel said, clinging to him. That made up his mind.

'OK. Miss Ann will be pleased to see you and so will a lot of other people.' He could always come back later and make sure Miguel wasn't still alive.

'Will we be able to have a wash and something nice to eat?' Rachel asked, sounding very like the little girl that she was.

'I'm sure Miss Ann will arrange hot soapy baths and a feast.'

At that Claire knew they were safe at last. Just as her sister had done, she put her arms around Walsh and wept against his chest.

31

As soon as Greeley arrived back in Elk Horn he rode to the marshal's house, anxious in case Detmeyer and Ann could be in danger, either from the gang members he was chasing after from the hideout or from the man who'd shot at him. He was even more anxious when he realized that no one was guarding the place, either front or back, and there was no answer to his knock.

It didn't look as if any trouble had happened there, but had someone managed to break in again?

'Mr Greeley.'

He turned. It was Mrs Hooper calling his name.

'What's going on?' he asked. 'Where's the marshal?'

'Much to my husband's annoyance, and Ann's too, he insisted on getting up this morning and going to his office stead of staying in bed like he should.'

Greeley grinned. 'Ain't that just like Sam not to do as he's told?'

'And Ann went with him.'

Just like her too, he thought with another grin. 'Bet Sam didn't like that'

'No,' Mrs Hooper said with her own answering smile. 'She insisted.'

'OK I'll go and see them. Got some things to tell Sam.'

'Any sign of the Baker girls, Mr Greeley?'

'I'm keeping my fingers crossed about them.'

⋆   ⋆   ⋆

Marshal Detmeyer was sitting in his chair behind his desk when Greeley got to the office. He didn't look too happy but Greeley couldn't tell if that was because he was in pain and regretted leaving his bed or because Ann was sitting across from him with a stern look of disapproval on her face, a pile of Wanted posters in front of her, while

Eddie Smith hovered in the background. Of course, it could also be to do with the fact that Ann's face lit up in a delighted smile when she saw Gus.

'What are you doing up and about, Sam?' Greeley said. 'Shouldn't you be in bed still?'

'Exactly what I told him,' Ann said.

'I'm fine,' Detmeyer growled.

'You don't look it.'

'Hell's bells, Greeley, quit fussing! I would be even better if these two would do as they were told. But Eddie won't go home and leave me by myself, thinks I can't cope or something. Nor will my daughter who, instead, is looking at posters of outlaws an' such. Which is not woman's work. She can be very obstinate when she likes.'

'Wonder who she gets that from?' Greeley accepted a mug of coffee from Eddie with a nod of thanks. He sat down on the edge of Detmeyer's desk.

Ann said, 'I've got to do something. These are pictures of wanted men, that's all. They can't harm me.'

'They detail what they're wanted for. It's not nice.'

'That can't hurt me either. Mr Greeley, did you find Claire and Rachel?' Her voice trembled; the girls weren't with Gus; please God he wouldn't say they were dead!

'No, but Henry Walsh is following what we believe is their trail.'

'They're alive then?' Ann's eyes lit up with hope.

'Looks that way.'

'Why didn't you go with Mr Walsh?'

'Because I was concerned for you.'

Greeley quickly told the other three of all that he and Walsh had done and found that morning, although he didn't go into detail about why the girls were being taken to Mexico: the two lawmen would realize why and Ann didn't need to know. He ended up by saying he'd been ambushed.

'Did you see who it was?' Detmeyer asked, sitting up straight and trying not to wince.

'Nope. But I followed his tracks

almost into Elk Horn. Lost 'em when he got to the road into town. I ain't sure if he was one of the gang returning to the hideout for some reason, or someone else.' Greeley frowned. 'Trouble is it's no good asking anyone if they've seen strangers hanging around. Any strangers would be taken for cowboys who'd just signed up on a spread.'

'Still, if you're right seems like we should be ready for trouble,' Detmeyer said. 'Ann, you must go home. Or better yet go to the Hoopers. Stay with them.'

'There's no must about it.'

'Your pa's right,' Greeley said. 'A man has already tried to kill him . . . '

'You shot him. He's no threat.'

'But someone else might try instead. You could be in danger if you stay here.'

'I could be in danger elsewhere. Besides, this is where Mr Walsh will likely bring Claire and Rachel. I want to see them again as soon as they arrive. Help them. They'll need comforting after going through goodness knows

hat. They've lost their family. I must
do all I can for them. They'll want to
see a friendly face, a girl, someone they
know, not more men they've hardly ever
spoken to.'

Greeley shrugged.

'Surely if anywhere is safe it's here in
the marshal's office where I'm pro-
tected by three well-armed men.' Ann
smiled sweetly. 'No, I'm sorry, Papa, Mr
Greeley, but I'm staying. My mind is
made up.'

Detmeyer sighed.

★ ★ ★

Claire groaned in relief as at long, long
last they neared Elk Horn. What would
happen to her and Rachel then, or who
would look after him she didn't know,
but they could stop being afraid. Walsh
glanced across at her and smiled.

'Marshal Detmeyer will want to learn
all that happened to you. Will you be
able to tell him?'

Claire nodded. 'We can also give him

names and descriptions of the bastard who attacked the farm. There were five of them, although the one who shot the marshal wasn't one of them. He was from Elk Horn. I think he's somehow involved with the man the others called the boss.'

'Ah! Do you know who that was?'

'No. Nate and the others only ever called him 'he' or 'the boss'. They were scared of him though. He came to the hideout one morning because he was angry with them, and he gave them orders.' Claire hesitated. 'One of which was to kill Marshal Detmeyer.'

'He's fine, sweetheart. A man did break into the marshal's house but Mr Greeley shot him and killed him.'

That must have been the one called Russ.

'Good, I'm glad he's dead.'

'It's even better that the marshal is all right,' Rachel said. 'He came to the farm to help us and we saw him get shot in the back. He fell to the ground and didn't move. The others laughed nd called him names.'

'But you didn't see this man, this boss?'

'We were shut up in the hut but I'd know his voice anywhere.'

'Me too,' Rachel added.

★ ★ ★

For the rest of the morning and into the afternoon, a string of townsfolk called at the marshal's office to find out how Detmeyer was and to learn what Greeley had to say.

As the time wore on Greeley got more and more worried about the marshal. He looked tired and in pain, his face was an ashen grey.

'Truth to tell I am hurting real bad,' he admitted. 'But I want to stay here at least until Walsh gets back. See if he has rescued the girls.'

'Papa.' Ann looked up from the Wanted poster she had just turned over.

There was a note of something, a warning, excitement maybe, in her voice, a glint in her eyes, that Greeley didn't understand. He thought it might be concern for her father, but that didn't seem right.

At the same moment the door opened and David and Will Preston came in.

Ann gave a little gasp and Greeley saw her quickly turn over the Wanted poster and place another on top of it. He glanced at her and she shook her head slightly.

'Hi, Marshal,' Preston said, all smiles and concern. 'We came to see how you were doing. What's been happening? Mr Greeley, good afternoon. Have you had any luck in finding the bastards . . . oh, sorry, Miss Detmeyer . . . er . . . the men responsible for the attack on the Baker farm?'

'Sort of,' Greeley said, not trying to hide his dislike of the two brothers.

'Is there anything me and Will can do to help? It seems wrong to just sit by and do nothing when our town is in danger.'

'There's no danger now that we now Apaches weren't responsible,' Greeley said.

Eddie Smith had wandered to the window; now he turned round and exclaimed,

'They're back! The girls! With Mr Walsh. They're safe and well.'

'Oh thank goodness!' Ann jumped up, ran to the door and opened it.

'Are you sure of your facts, Mr Greeley?' Preston said.

'As sure as sure can be.'

Outside the marshal's office Walsh helped Claire and Rachel down off the horse. All three stepped up on to the sidewalk. The door opened and Ann came rushing out.

Suddenly Claire came to a halt.

'What's the matter, sweetheart?'

'That's one of them!' Claire cried, pointing at Will. 'He's the one who shot Marshal Detmeyer. And the other one, I know his voice. That's the boss!'

32

Everything happened very quickly.

Greeley was already going into a crouch and drawing his gun from its holster.

At the same time, Preston yelled something and began to draw his own gun while Ann screamed in shock.

Out on the sidewalk Walsh saw the excited gleam in Will's eyes as the man turned towards his accusers.

'Watch out!' he yelled and shoved Claire and Rachel out of the way, knocking them to the ground.

'What the hell?' Detmeyer said. 'Ann!' There was panic in his voice, for she was in the doorway quite near to Will. 'Get down.'

Will swung towards the girl and fired even as she screamed again and jumped to one side. The bullet smacked into the sidewalk.

Eddie Smith cried out in alarm. Preston

hot him in the shoulder, sending him falling to the floor with a heavy thump.

'Eddie.' Ann called his name. She would have gone to him but Walsh caught her arm, holding her back.

Meanwhile Greeley had dived behind Eddie's desk as Preston shot at him — four, five times. Quick and accurate.

Will paused, looking back at his brother. Grinning he raised his gun to finish off Eddie, who could do nothing to defend himself. He never made it. Detmeyer grabbed hold of the shotgun he kept under his desk and let go with both barrels.

The noise was deafening in the confines of the small office. Hit full in the chest, Will flew backwards out of the door, to land on his back in the dust by Walsh's feet, his chest a mess of blood and shredded skin. He was dead before he hit the ground.

Claire pulled Rachel out of the way, cuddling her close so she wouldn't have to see.

As Will was killed, David Preston let

out a cry of anguish and hate. He
turned on Detmeyer.

'You bastard!'

Greeley jumped up and fired before
the man could get off his shot. His first
bullet struck Preston in the side, spin-
ning him round, the second hit him in
the head. He went down, tried to struggle
to his feet, but collapsed back, his eyes
open and staring unseeingly at the ceil-
ing.

'He dead?' Detmeyer asked shakily,
standing up.

Greeley nodded. 'So's the other one.'

In the sudden quiet, little could be
heard but Eddie moaning and, from
outside, a sobbing Rachel being com-
forted by her sister and Walsh. Ann, her
eyes wide and her face white with fear,
came back in the office to kneel by the
deputy.

'Eddie, are you all right? Eddie?'

'He'll be OK, honey,' Detmeyer said
to her, pulling her up and gathering her
in his arms, while she clung to him,
trembling all over. 'He was hit in the

shoulder. Hurt for a while is all. Someone will go for the doctor.'

People were emerging from all around to find out what was going on. A shootout in the middle of Elk Horn's Main Street in the middle of the afternoon? It was unheard of.

Detmeyer looked at his daughter wryly.

'You see what a good job it was that your good old dad decided to come to his office, so that he could save the day.'

Ann smiled a little. She didn't point out that if he hadn't been there then the Preston brothers wouldn't have been either. As far as she was concerned her father was a hero. As, of course, was Mr Greeley.

Detmeyer glanced at Greeley. 'What the hell was all that about?'

'This, I think.' Greeley picked up the Wanted poster that Ann had been looking at when the brothers came into the office.

'Let's see.'

It read:

WANTED
Dead or Alive
David & William Pressley
for murder, bank robbery and other outrages in Wichita, Dodge City & Abilene, Kansas.
Reward: $50 each.

There followed an accurate description of the men who had called themselves David and Will Preston.

'But, hell, Sam! I'll only claim the reward for shooting David. As you're a lawman and can't accept reward money because you're just doing your duty, the other fifty dollars can go to Claire and Rachel.'

33

'I'm glad it was the Preston brothers who were behind everything that happened and not Jack and Josephine,' Melissa said later that night. She and Greeley were curled up together in her bed. 'I know they're a strange pair and Jack is mean and ill-spirited but I wouldn't like to think of them being capable of doing something like that.'

'It also had to be someone with intelligence, or perhaps cunning is a better word, to come up with the idea and to get others to take most of the risks.' Greeley stroked her hair. 'Not that it's done any of them any good. The brothers are dead now, as are the men they hired.'

Melissa sighed. 'It's awful to think innocent, hardworking people were killed just because the Prestons hoped to buy up land cheaply.'

'Somehow I don't think they would ever have actually bought land, let alone started a ranch or a farm. They liked causing trouble and killing too much to ever be able to settle down, however much they thought they could.'

Melissa smiled. 'Jack and Josephine aren't going to do so either. They've decided it's safer to stay here in town. The two Baker girls — Gus, are they really all right? They weren't hurt, were they? Not . . . you know . . . by the men, I mean?'

'No, thankfully. They were very brave. Especially Claire. She was determined not to let them get away with what they'd done. Even so, I guess it'll take them both a long time and much sympathy to get over their ordeal. They're resting at Doc Hooper's at the moment. Mrs Hooper is taking good care of them.'

'What will happen to them?'

'I understand there's an aunt and uncle and plenty of cousins back East somewhere. They've been told, and in a while someone is coming out to fetch the girls and take them back with them to a new home.'

'That's good news. At least they won't be on their own but will have family around.'

Unlike me: the words seemed to hang in the air.

'And they'll have fifty dollars to take with them too.'

'How is Eddie?'

Greeley grinned. 'Like Sam said, he wasn't badly hurt. But he's making the most of it because Ann is so concerned about him and has insisted on helping to nurse him better. Sam is pleased because, at least for the moment, Ann has transferred her affections from me to Eddie, although he's not all that pleased, because Eddie is a lowly deputy.

'He's sure she can do better than that, as well as not have the worry of being married to a lawman. Perhaps after seeing her father hurt so badly she'll come to realize that as well.'

Melissa smiled back. 'He shouldn't fret. Ann is only young. She's got plenty of time to fall in and out of love several times before she makes up her mind about who she wants to marry.'

A sad look came into her eyes, as it had when she mentioned the family of the Baker girls. Something was wrong.

'What's the matter, sweetheart?'

Melissa sat up. 'Oh, Gus, Roger is getting better and as soon as his hands heal properly he's going to leave Elk Horn. He's decided to try his luck in Tucson.' She bit her lip.

Melissa was used to the men in her life coming and going; that couldn't be all there was to it. It wasn't.

'He's asked me to go with him. He's asked me to marry him.'

A bolt of pain and distress shot through Greeley. He'd lose her. Never see her again. How could he bear that?

'I want to leave this life and be a respectable woman at last. I want to have children. Do you mind? I won't go if you tell me not to.'

Of course he minded. He minded a helluva lot. He'd always mind. But how could he stop her? Right then with his precarious life as a bounty hunter, settling down into marriage and having a family wasn't something he could offer her. So he smiled as best he could.

'Melissa, sweetheart,' he said, 'I wish you well, I really do, with all my heart. You deserve some happiness.'

The next day he'd go to the marshal's office and see if any information had come in about the man who'd killed his father; because, despite whoever or whatever he lost, he couldn't, wouldn't give up his life until he'd found him, caught him and shot the bastard dead.

We do hope that you have enjoyed reading this large print book.

Did you know that all of our titles are available for purchase?

We publish a wide range of high quality large print books including:
Romances, Mysteries, Classics
General Fiction
Non Fiction and Westerns

Special interest titles available in large print are:
The Little Oxford Dictionary
Music Book, Song Book
Hymn Book, Service Book

Also available from us courtesy of Oxford University Press:
Young Readers' Dictionary
(large print edition)
Young Readers' Thesaurus
(large print edition)

For further information or a free brochure, please contact us at:
Ulverscroft Large Print Books Ltd.,
The Green, Bradgate Road, Anstey,
Leicester, LE7 7FU, England.
Tel: (00 44) **0116 236 4325**
Fax: (00 44) **0116 234 0205**

DEVINE'S MISSION

I. J. Parnham

When Lachlan McKinley raids Fairmount Town's bank, the bounty on his head attracts plenty of manhunters — but everyone who goes after him ends up dead. When bounty hunter Jonathon Lynch, Lachlan's stepbrother, joins the hunt, he soon discovers that all is not as it seems, and Lachlan may in fact be innocent. Worse, US Marshal Jake Devine is also after Lachlan. Devine is more likely to destroy the peace than to keep it, so can Jonathon bring the guilty to justice before Devine does his worst?

PERIL ON THE OREGON TRAIL

Billy Hall

Hannah Henford, travelling west aboard a steamer, meets the reticent young Andrew Stevenson, who captures her heart with his bravery when the boat docks and they embark upon the Oregon Trail. Jeremiah Smith, a mysterious and adventurous mountain man, discovers Hannah alone and takes her in search of wild turkeys. She cannot help but be charmed by Jeremiah, but he may not be all that he seems. In Arapaho territory, Andrew will be needed again: in pursuit of Hannah, he will face peril on the Oregon Trail.

THE VIGILANCE COMMITTEE WAR

Bill Sheehy

A gang of vigilantes calling themselves the Vigilance Committee are preventing part of the Indian Territory from becoming a state, and former Texas Rangers Buck Armstrong and Louie Lewis are being paid by local businesses to bring them in. Making their job difficult is the fact that most of the area's ranchers don't care, or approve of the hangings carried out by the Committee. When the pards get too close to Committee members, Louie himself ends up at the end of a hangman's noose . . .

ALONG THE TONTO RIM

Will DuRey

Dick Lazarus and his gang are feared on both sides of the Rio Grande. Lazarus's increasingly daring crimes see him raid the ranchero of the Robles family in Mexico, stealing a herd of horses and taking a hostage — Luis Robles — who should fetch a hefty ransom. Dan Calloway, owner of the stolen herd and Luis's friend, is determined to rescue Luis and regain his possessions. Ignoring the warnings, and with an unexpected ally on his side, he pursues Lazarus across the Rio Grande, and along the Tonto Rim . . .

HARD RIDE TO GLORY

Harry Jay Thorn

Having survived the horrors of battle, Griffin Boone is happy in his Wyoming valley; he has his Arrowhead ranch, his close friends, and a job as a part-time deputy sheriff. But the peace is threatened by Heck Thomas and his outlaw crew of gunfighters and vagabond thieves. Ride with Boone to the ruins of Glory, a ghost town in the foothills of the Big Horn Mountains, where past meets present in a blaze of gunfire. Griffin Boone is a quiet, unassuming man — but you cross him at your peril!